Yvonne has been writing stories and poems from a young age. She has had a full-length novel and a children's book published as well as a number of poems and articles for local magazines. She was a former Chief Laboratory Scientist for the Medical Research Council and has written papers for medical and scientific journals. Yvonne lives in Hertfordshire, spending her time writing and painting.

My thanks to Pierre Bosdet for his constant help and for sorting out my computer problems. To my friends, and family for their encouragement.

Yvonne Stirling

A RIGHT TO LIFE

AUSTIN MACAULEY PUBLISHERS™

LONDON * CAMBRIDGE * NEW YORK * SHARJAH

A CIP catalogue record for this title is available from the British Library.

ISBN 9781035832798 (Paperback)
ISBN 9781035832804 (ePub e-book)

www.austinmacauley.com

First Published 2024
Austin Macauley Publishers Ltd®
1 Canada Square
Canary Wharf
London
E14 5AA

My thanks to Orlando Rutter, Head of Outreach and Understanding, Dartmoor National Park Authority, for sharing his great knowledge of the Dartmoor National Park.

Chapter 1

On a warm summer's evening, four friends approaching middle age, something they were reluctant to admit to, sat in a pub garden chattering and laughing, catching up on the news. They had not met for some time so there was a lot to say. Friends from schooldays, they had scattered into various careers but had always kept in touch. With a glass of wine in her hand, Jennie looked across at Alexa and said, 'I read something about you in a posh newspaper the other day, something about you rescuing a girl from Dartmoor.'

'Oh, that is a bit of an exaggeration,' Alexa replied.

'Well, come on. Tell all.'

Alexa hesitated. 'This girl got lost on the moor and Philip, a policeman who knows the area, helped her find her way back to her family. It's all a long time ago now.'

'Why didn't you tell us? We're your friends. We always share.'

'I couldn't tell you.'

'Why not?'

'It would have caused great trouble for the family.'

'Well tell us now.'

Alexa moved her wineglass around in her hands, hesitating. 'Alright. I'll give you an outline, but not all the details. I would not wish to put anyone at risk.'

The other three girls leaned forward over the table eager to hear.

'Wait,' said Jennie. 'I'll get us another drink first. Same again?'

'Yes please,' they replied in unison.

Jennie came back with four glasses and four packets of crisps balanced on a tray. Distributing them around, she grinned at Alexa. 'OK, let us begin.'

'It all began with a girl running towards my car when I was held up by a storm in a layby on the A30, on my way to Cornwall,' said Alexa. She recounted briefly what had happened, the battles with the local Council, the families involved and the fascinating history as to why this sorry state of affairs had come about.

'Well, there you are. That's the bones of it.'

'Fascinating,' said Sue. The trio had sat staring at Alexa with absolute interest and amazement. It was rare for them to be quiet that long.

Diana, the fourth member of the gang, piped up, 'You should write a book.' The other three nodded in agreement.

And so, she did. "A Right to Life".

The first streak of dawn light stretched across the sky as she picked up the wicker basket containing an angry, yowling cat and made her way to the car. She was determined to be on her way before the morning rush hour started. She put the basket on the back seat next to the silent one already there and firmly locked the car door.

The two cats were of vastly different temperaments. Following a session in the pet sanctuary waiting to be selected, Fluff, a sweet-natured animal, just seemed grateful for a home and quietly consented to anything asked of her. Ivan, a Russian Blue, was a completely different kettle of fish. A handsome beast with a long pedigree he felt entitled to demand anything he wanted. Arrogant and noisy, he was now loudly objecting to being shut in a basket and was letting the world know he was being badly treated. He had been her father's cat and was spoilt and overindulged. But Father was gone now, and Ivan was having to adjust to ordinary living.

'Oh, do stop that noise,' she said. 'You're going on holiday. You know you'll like it when we get there.' As if he understood what she was saying to him.

She got into the driver's seat and paused to collect her thoughts. Yes, she had locked the front door. Her clothes, paints, books were in the boot along with enough food for herself and the cats to last a couple of days.

Dear old Mrs Nicholls, her next-door neighbour, had happily agreed to keep an eye on the house while she was away. She liked doing it. Besides doing a bit of dusting she watched the television, making herself at home in the armchair, switching on the electric fire. She enjoyed, as she called it, "a little break"; it was a situation agreeable to both parties. The house would be immaculate on homecoming and Mrs N would be amply rewarded with Cornish pasties and clotted cream.

Alexa tossed the keys into the cup tray, pressed the starter then pressed down on the accelerator, gripped the steering wheel, leant her head on it and started to cry. This was the first journey to Cornwall without Daniel. They had always shared the driving, laughing, joking, keeping each other alert, but he too was gone, died of cancer last year. It had not been a great romance, more of a caring, sharing relationship of two people who needed each other. It had worked and twice a year they went down to the cottage Alexa had surprisingly inherited from an aunt she had not known too well.

It was Daniel's idea to take the cats, a risky venture, but infinitely preferable to coming home and collecting two thin, unhappy animals from the cattery. They took to it like ducks to water going out over the cliffs to bring home mice, birds and on one occasion a young rabbit.

Alexa raised her head, dried her eyes and announced, 'O.K. kids and with no dissenting comments from the cat baskets, put the car into gear and drove off westward with the sky behind her in the east becoming ever lighter and now diffused with the rosy colours of dawn.'

'I have decided to avoid the horrible motorways, skirt Slough, go through Windsor Great Park and pick up the A303,' she announced. It was better to talk to the cats than think of other problems. 'Just drive,' she said. 'Time to think about all this later.'

With the hours and the distance moving on, she found herself passing through areas of grassland, small hamlets with just a few cottages and glimpses of brightly coloured front gardens.

'This is nice,' she said. 'Oh look. There's Stonehenge,' as the great ancient circle of stones came into view. Even from this distance, it had a mystic quality about it. 'I must pay a closer visit sometime.' She was talking to the cats again. 'We'll stop soon, and I can get some breakfast and you two can take a walk as soon as we see a suitable café.'

A few miles further on, she saw a place with a car park and surrounding area of grass. 'OK, this will do.'

Taking a sharp left turn, she drove to the furthest corner, cut the engine and stretched her legs in front of her. Getting out of the car, she opened the rear door, leaned in and carefully opened up the nearest basket. Quickly grasping the lead, she wound it round her hand and extracted a sleepy looking Ivan. 'Come on, sweetheart, walkies.' Putting him on the ground, she relocked the car door and led him over to the lawn bordered by a hedge. He stopped to do a wee, scratching at the grass in a cover up job. Pulling at the lead, he strode off over the grass. A little girl called out, 'Mummy. There's a pussycat.'

'Where are you taking him?' the lady asked.

'We are going to Cornwall on holiday. There's another one in the car. Come over and I'll get her out.' They followed her and watched as she put Ivan back in his basket and brought out Fluff.

'You can stroke her if you like,' she said to the little girl. 'She won't mind.'

'Mummy, she's lovely. Can I have a cat?' as Fluff allowed herself to be stroked and kissed.

'We had better let the lady get on.' Turning to Alexa. 'Do you have far to go?'

'I have a cottage on the Helford River.'

The lady gave her a quizzical look as though to say, *What is a youngish woman (well, coming up to middle age) doing driving to the end of the country with two cats in tow?*

She either thinks I am dotty or a witch.

'My husband died young in a car accident.' She felt compelled to defend herself. She refrained from saying my mother, my father, my sister and now my dear friend Daniel have all departed. She had begun to feel like an omen, a harbinger of doom.

'I am sorry,' the lady replied and looked it. 'You are very brave. Good luck.'

Alexa nodded and headed back to the car, the faithful Fluff trotting demurely alongside her. With the cats safely stowed, she walked over to the café and ordered coffee and a sandwich.

'Daniel. I need you now. I didn't realise it would be so hard on my own. Well, we have made it halfway; we may as well go on.' She felt tearful, gulped down some of the coffee and picking up her sandwich, got up and hurried out.

Back in the car, she took a couple more mouthfuls of coffee.

'Heavens, don't let me cry now,' she pleaded to herself, started the engine and resumed her journey. 'Please don't let it rain,' she prayed. 'We were doing so well.' The countryside which had looked so beautiful in the sunshine now looked grey and uninviting with a mist hanging low, blotting out the view. Worse still it was starting to rain. Large drops hit the windscreen. Turning on the wipers they moved leisurely at first then speeded up faster and faster as the rain came crashing down.

The sky had clouded over, the sun had gone In.

'Gosh. I can't see where I'm going,' she muttered. Turning on the headlights, she moved her face closer to the windscreen in an attempt to see the road. Driving very slowly, she at last spied a layby and thankfully signalled left and drove in.

The noise on the roof of the car was deafening; she could hardly hear herself think let alone see.

'We are going to Cornwall. Right kids. This weather can't last forever.'

Eventually, the crashing rain softened to a drizzle. She looked out across the moor. The sky was growing lighter, the mist not so dense. The outline of a large tree appeared with its branches swaying in the wind except that the wind had dropped. She turned to look the other way but nothing else was moving. Looking ahead again she saw that the tree was coming nearer still swaying and the branches waving to and fro. Later she learned that the mist over the moor can exaggerate the size of a moving object.

Am I going nuts? she thought when the tree turned into a person and came running towards her. 'It's a woman,' she said. A youngish girl wearing a long dress and a shawl around her shoulders appeared. She was soaked to the skin, the water running off her, her hair hanging down in long rats' tails.

Alexa sounded the horn to attract her attention. The girl visibly jumped and stared at the car as though she had never seen anything like it. Now that she was closer, she could see that the girl looked terrified, her eyes wide open and staring.

Lowering the window a bit, Alexa called, 'Do you want a lift? Where are you going?'

The girl still stood like a statue.

'Get into the car.' She released the catch, leant over and opened the rear door. 'Come on. You are letting the rain in.'

Still, the girl stood immobile. Alexa was getting a bit fed up. 'Well. Do you want a lift or not?' the irritation sounding in her voice. 'I haven't got all day and you are letting the rain in the car.'

Suddenly, the girl made a gazelle-like leap and landed in the car pushing aside the cat baskets whose occupants made their annoyance and fright known by miaowing loudly. 'You're as confused as I am,' she said to the cats. 'Shut the door, please.' The girl still sat there and Alexa, with difficulty, leant over, shut the door and locked it. Thank Heaven for modern cars.

Releasing her seatbelt, she turned right around and faced the girl. 'Look, love. I can't help you if you won't talk to me. Where do you want to go?' No answer.

She looked like a frightened fawn; her face chalky white, her eyes, a dark brown, almost jumping out of her head.

'What is your name?' The girl remained rigid. 'Are you running away from something or someone?' Tears started in the girl's eyes and dripped down her cheeks. 'I guess that must be it, though what or who I have no idea,' she surmised. 'Here. You are soaked. You must be cold.' She turned the heater up to maximum and taking off her anorak handed it over. 'Wrap this around you.'

The girl took it and laid it across her.

'The problem is what to do with you.' *Oh Lord, don't I have problems enough without this?* she thought. 'Well,' she said, 'I will drop you at the police station in the next town and let them sort it out.'

She refastened her seatbelt, pressed the starter and moved off having decided it would be hopeless trying to get the girl to put on her seatbelt.

Now I'll probably get picked up by the police and get fined, she thought.

The girl squealed as the car moved off. *At least, she can speak. But has she never seen or been in a car?*

'Well. I am just going to drive on and hope you will tell me when you want to get out.'

Alexa drove on bounded by the moor, through small towns and hamlets with no word from the girl in the back. At one point, she pulled off the road, turned round to face her passenger and said quite firmly, 'I am trying to help you. Where are you going? Right,' she said as no response came. 'I am going to take you to a police station. And as the only one I am familiar with in Exeter is near the cathedral and it is so difficult to park, we will go on to the bypass avoiding Honiton, skirt Truro and on to Falmouth.'

She looked longingly at the turnoff for Constantine and Porth Abbas and drove down the road known as the Moor into the main shopping street leading up from the harbour, looking for the police station.

'Well, where is it then? I am sure I heard somewhere that it was along here,' she muttered.

She pulled up in the road, parked and looked around. The street was almost deserted then she saw someone just ahead. She lowered the window and called out, 'Excuse me. Can you tell me where the police station is?' He came over to the car. He looked like a fisherman, wearing navy trousers, navy sweater and a peaked cap at a saucy angle. He looked friendly and smiled.

'I'm looking for the police station. I thought it was in this street.'

'You're going the wrong way. Good Heavens lass. How long since you been to Falmouth? I think there was one long ago, but not in my lifetime. It's up on Dracaena Street. Turn the car around, keep going along, then ask again.' Suddenly noticing the girl in the back of the car, 'Is she alright? She do look rather ill. Perhaps you need the hospital.'

'She's lost and not well. I am hoping the police will help find her family.'

The man took another look at the girl who, white-faced and rigid, stared straight ahead. 'She looks as though she could do with some help and so do you.'

She drove off. 'What a fool. I must have passed it.'

Having eventually found the police station, she parked and said to the girl, 'Are you coming in with me? Well at least tell me your name.' With still no reply, she got out of the car, flicked the key to lock it, and walked into the station. *I hope to Heaven she doesn't escape. She can't seem to manage opening and shutting the doors so I think she will stay there. Actually, I wish she would escape then I wouldn't have to deal with her. Oh, don't be nasty. The kid is scared out of her wits.*

Noisy chaos greeted her as a couple of policemen tried to deal with some obviously drunken louts, shouting and protesting.

'Get them in the cells and let them sober up,' came a voice from beyond. 'We'll sort them out later.'

'Sorry about that. Yes, young lady. What can I do for you?' He sounded a kindly man with a strong Cornish accent; he looked worn out.

'Today's youth,' she said.

'Indeed. We get a lot of drink and drug problems here.'

'And I thought Falmouth was a nice quiet town.'

'Used to be,' he replied. 'How can I help you?'

She felt suddenly ridiculous. She had a soaking wet young girl who refused to speak or get out of the car. Also, two upset cats who had been shut in their baskets all day and needed to be fed. She felt tears welling up. 'I'll get us a cup of tea and you can tell me all about it,' said the policeman. 'Steve,' he called out. 'Bring a couple of cups of tea and then take over the desk for a bit.'

'Right Gov. Sugar?'

She shook her head. 'No thank you.'

'Yes in mine,' the policeman called back. 'You should know that by now.' He sat opposite Alexa at the table. 'You look upset. What's all this about?'

Alexa recounted the tale of the girl appearing out of the mist. 'I was just trying to be nice. She was soaking wet, and I asked her to get in the car and said I would drop her off where she wanted. She stood there staring at the car as though it was a spaceship and finally got in. She is wearing very old-fashioned clothes. Do you think she is a mental patient? Now she won't tell me her name, where she has come from, or where she wants to go.' Alexa felt she was going to cry.

The police sergeant looked at her sympathetically. 'Perhaps she has had a row with her family and is running away. But the moor is a funny old place. I worked up that way for some years and learned how mysterious it is. There are isolated houses, tiny hamlets and, some say, small communities living in the lonely parts or the combes; those deep forested hidden valleys where people can hide from the police or the tax inspectors. Even the rangers who work on the moor are sometimes surprised by an area they haven't seen before. What with those great granite blocks, winding paths that seem to go nowhere and the constant mists that suddenly drop-down obscuring everything. Sadly, many a hiker has lost his way and a number have died over the years.'

Steve brought in two mugs of tea. Alexa drank hers gratefully, reminding herself she had not eaten or drunk for many hours.

'Well. All that doesn't solve your problem, does it. Where is she now?'

'In the car outside in the car park. I don't think she could work out how to get out.'

Perhaps she has escaped from somewhere and run away, she thought. *I know I am horrible, but it would solve my problem. Remember Alexa. Never offer a stranger a lift even if she is a soaking wet young girl.*

'Well. We had better take a look at her then,' said the sergeant. 'Follow me.'

The girl was sitting quite still, wrapped in Alexa's anorak.

'Open the door and I will see if she will talk to me.'

Alexa did as requested and the girl shrank back against the seat as though trying to disappear into it. She looked up at the sergeant with huge, frightened eyes.

'Hello love,' softening his voice. 'Will you tell me your name?' Total silence. 'Well, you can't stay in there, can you?' Turning to Alexa, he said, 'You've got a right one there. Come back into the station and I'll ring Social Services and see if they can find her a bed for the night.'

The sergeant dismissed Steve, reached for the phone and pressed a key. 'Hello Irene. I have a problem for you.' The voice was companionable; they had obviously spoken before.

'Another one?' she said. 'What now?'

'I need a bed for a young girl we know nothing about.'

'Well, that's a good start. You know nothing?'

'Well, only that she came off the moor, got into a car and refuses to speak or move.'

'She sounds like a mental patient to me.'

'That's what occurred to me, but I have the feeling she is running away from something.'

'Well, you know a lot more about the moor than I do. There are some very odd people living there. Anyway, this a pointless conversation because we haven't a bed anywhere. You know what it's like. They start applying early afternoon and it's now coming up to five o'clock so there is nothing left.'

'And you want to go home.'

'Yep. I don't know why I do this job. Why don't you try the Help Trust; they're pretty helpful. Oh dear, sorry; that's an awful joke.'

'I'll forgive you. Good idea. I'll try the Trust. Talk soon.'

'When you want something,' she laughed. 'Bye Phil,' she said and rang off.

He looked up at Alexa. 'Nothing doing with Social Services. They suggest trying the Help Trust. They deal with young offenders recently released from prison, boys and girls. I'm sure they will help if they can. Good people the Help Trust.'

So, with more instructions, she eventually found the Help Trust and went into the office. A gentle voice asked how she could help and Alexa once more recounted her story.

'Oh dear, all the beds are taken. Most of our customers are here for a couple of weeks until we try to get them settled into a more permanent job.' She paused for a moment and then as if struck by divine inspiration looked up at Alexa. 'I suppose you couldn't give her a bed for the night, could you? Bring her back in the morning and we will definitely help her.'

'What?' Alexa almost reeled back with shock. 'No. I can't,' she almost shouted. *Haven't I done enough? She is not my responsibility. I was just trying to help. I have been travelling since the early hours of the morning. I have two upset, hungry animals in the car, and I want to get to my cottage. This was*

supposed to be a holiday and it is turning out to be more like a prison sentence.
She turned away and burst into tears.

'I didn't mean to upset you. Just for one night?'

'Surely that would be illegal? Like kidnapping her.'

Alexa dried her eyes on a tissue and sniffed. The Help Trust lady was on the phone.

'Phil,' she said. 'we are still trying to sort out this girl from the Moor. Would the nice young lady be allowed to take her home for one night? We honestly have nowhere to place her.' All roads seemed to lead to Phil.

'Well,' the sergeant replied. 'I can't arrest the girl for being lost. So, it's OK if she will do it. A bit unfair on her.'

'Thanks Phil. Goodnight.'

Alexa found herself giving in. She mostly did, programmed by an overbearing, dominant father. 'Alright,' she said. 'One night.' At this stage, she was prepared to do almost anything just to get the animals home and fed.

She signed a couple of forms and left the office to the sounds of the officer praising her goodness.

Getting back into the car, she called out to the miserable cats. 'Won't be long now. I am sorry, darlings. Not you,' she said nastily to the immobile girl in the back, not that she had moved or displayed any interest.

Driving out of Falmouth and into the familiar lanes and high hedges still bright with the last of the wildflowers, such a feature of this part of the countryside, she finally felt as though she was in Cornwall. Having travelled the world, nowhere else had she seen the display of beauty and colour that appeared here annually. For a while, she forgot the girl sitting in the back or the problems to come.

After turning off for Constantine, she started looking for the two white gate posts signalling the beginning of the track that led over the fields and down to the farm and the small white cottage that stood above the Helford River. She slowed down and took in the magnificent view where the creek widened out past Durgan and on to the open sea. It was high water, and she could make out the boats rocking on the tide as it washed into its furthest inland point. Opposite lay Frenchman's Creek, the basis for a wondrous tale of pirates by Daphne du Maurier. It was scarcely deep enough to get a rowing boat up there, but with a fair wind and a great imagination it made for an exciting story. 'Stupid animal!'

she yelled as a rabbit scampered across the road bringing her back to the present day.

'Oh, I love this place. Bless you, Great Aunt Alice, for leaving it to me.'

She drove on, the track going downhill now, past the hay barns and levelling out in front of a five barred gate. Having opened it up, she moved on to a concrete standing and stopped the engine. She paused for a moment to look down the creek once again. The sky had faded to pale grey, the trees lining both sides of the creek had lost their deep green colour and begun to merge with the whole scene.

'Well. Can't sit here admiring the view. Come on, kids; let's get you in and fed,' and getting out and opening the rear door, pulled out the two cat baskets and made her way up to the door of the cottage.

It felt warm when she opened up. The agent who looked after the place had thoughtfully put on the heating so the water would be hot as well.

Going back to the car, she collected a box of cat food, made sure the girl was locked in, took the baskets into the bathroom and let the cats out. They stretched their legs stiffly then climbed out onto the floor. Putting two plates of food and a bowl of water on the floor, she shut the door and left them.

'Poor little devils. It wasn't meant to be like this,' she muttered.

Now for the girl. I wish I knew what her name was; it would make it easier. She went back out to the car. 'Come on,' she said. 'You have to come indoors now. You need to get those wet clothes off and have something to eat.' The girl still sat staring ahead.

Obviously polite requests were not going to work. Be firm but kind.

Alexa opened the door, got hold of the girl's arm and said, 'Get out. You can't stay here all night.'

A voice came through the hedge. 'You alright, my love? Got trouble with the cats?' It was Jen, the farmer's wife. 'Do you want some help?'

'Can you come around, Jen?' she called back. 'I could do with some help.'

Jen came from a prestigious family going back a long way. She was well educated but had managed to keep a Cornish edge to the way she spoke despite the school's best effort to erase it. She had married a local farmer and done her share of the work along with bringing up two children. Her husband had recently died so she had the lot to deal with.

She managed a herd of cows and a flock of sheep with expertise. She had even stood up to the temper of Ferdie the bull. If anyone could deal with this girl, it would be Jen.

'Where did she come from?'

'I don't know. Tell you about it later. Just help me get her indoors, will you?'

'Who is she? She looks right odd to me.'

'I don't know who she is. I was asked to look after her.'

Jen put her head in the car and shouted in a loud voice straight into the girl's face. 'Get out of the car.'

She jumped, turned her face with those huge, terrified eyes and looked at Jen, who grabbed her arm, pulled her out, led her up to the door and shoved her in.

'My God. That's progress,' said Alexa. 'Thanks Jen.'

'She's wet and where did she get those odd clothes? She looks as though she's walked out of a jumble sale.'

'I'll tell you all about it tomorrow. If you could help me remove those clothes, dry her off. I'll give her some soup or she'll die of pneumonia or we will both die of hunger.'

'Where are the cats?'

'I have shut them in the bathroom with their food. Switch the fire on and sit her in the chair, will you? Here, she can have my dressing gown.' Alexa undid a bag she had dragged in from the car.

Jen managed to get the wet clothes off, dried her with a towel and put Alexa's dressing gown on her. 'I've got to go up to Top Farm and feed some calves now. I'll see you in the morning. Good luck.'

'Thanks Jen.'

Alexa emptied a couple of tins of soup into a saucepan and heated it up. Pouring some into a dish, she buttered a slice of bread and put it on the table.

Going over to the girl, she touched her arm. 'Come and eat. Now.'

The girl shrank back as though she was about to be hit. Alexa grabbed her arm and pulled her across the room and manoeuvred her into a chair at the table. Pushing a spoon into her hand, she commanded, 'Eat,' and picking up her own spoon she started to drink the soup.

The girl suddenly started to drink the soup making a disgusting, slurping noise and finished the contents rapidly, followed greedily by the slice of bread. 'My gosh. She must have been hungry. I wonder when she last ate and how long she had been out on the moor?' wondered Alexa.

Having encouraged the girl back to the chair by the fire, Alexa was going up to the bedrooms when she suddenly rushed back into the kitchen, locked the door, put the key in her pocket thinking, *I can't risk her getting out. I hope she doesn't investigate the windows. Perhaps she might drop off to sleep.*

The beds had been made up and the rooms were quite warm. Although it was still the end of summer, the cold and damp seeped into the thick stone walls if the cottage was left uninhabited for too long. She would put her visitor in the small room where there were two single beds and bring up a hot water bottle later.

Turning to the main room, she hesitated before going in. The double bed was covered with a coloured quilt; a vase of flowers standing on the chest of drawers. The last time she was here, Daniel was still alive. Everything had happened so quickly, dead in just a few months. They had been so happy here and now I have to get into that bed and sleep alone. No faint snoring or comfortable body to curl up to.

She went back downstairs.

Weariness had suddenly attacked her, and it took a great effort to collect the dishes, take them out to the kitchen and wash them up. Dragging out the cat litter from under the sink, she tipped some into a tray and put it on the floor. Knowing that the girl would be forced to use the toilet before long, she scooped up the cats and brought them into the kitchen.

'You will have to stay in here for the night.' She said. 'I dare not let you out till the morning. You must be very upset with all the carry on today. Here I go again. Talking to the cats.'

Shutting the kitchen door, she made her way across the lounge, sat on the settee opposite the television, picked up the control and flicked it on. The silver blue light heralding garish adverts appeared. The girl stared at this apparition and sat transfixed. Alexa almost laughed; it was the biggest response from her so far. It must be like me meeting E.T. or Doctor Who.

The outside light was fading, it was now around seven p.m. *I'll try and get her into bed by about eight o'clock. She must be completely physically exhausted, and so am I. With all the mental trauma she has suffered today she should sleep, and I can have a rest and think about tomorrow. Now all I have to do is to persuade her to climb the stairs.*

After a while, she looked over at the girl. 'Bed for you. I'll show you to the toilet then we'll go upstairs. Come along.' *I hope she knows how to use a toilet. Perhaps she digs a hole like an animal. Oh, don't be nasty, Alexa.*

'Do you understand?' said Alexa, staring straight at her. 'You need to go to bed.' For the first time she looked back at Alexa as though she was not the witch of the wood and didn't want to roast her over a fire. She stood up and allowed herself to be pushed towards the stairs.

The climbing of the staircase needed a bit of persuasion, but they eventually made it to the small room. Alexa pulled the curtains and switched on the bedside lamp. Holding up a garment, like a long cotton T-shirt, Alexa indicated that she should put it on. With her back to Alexa, she took off the dressing gown and stood naked. Where had she come from? Eventually, she put on the nightshirt.

Alexa inspected the clothes, now dried off, she had carried up to the bedroom, with interest.

They were all handmade, sewn with tiny, neat stitches. A good seamstress had made these. The pants were incredible, like long pantaloons, almost Victorian, a far cry from the bikinis and thongs which are almost the norm these days. A long petticoat and something my old aunt called a bust bodice completed the ensemble. She could have been dressed for a fancy dress party. Surely this was not every-day wear? She pulled back the bedclothes and indicated to the girl that she should get in. She eventually concurred and was half asleep when Alexa covered her up. A few minutes later, heavy breathing ensued, and she was out for the count.

Chapter 2

When Alexa opened the kitchen door, the cats rushed into the lounge, Ivan winning the race, stretching himself out in his usual selfish style full length on the carpet in front of the fire. Fluff with grace and good manners settled for sitting on her lap.

Alexa started to doze off but couldn't allow herself the luxury. She had to plan for tomorrow. She literally shook her head to keep herself awake. It had been a day of doings things; who to talk to, where to go. *Now she had time to think. How have I got myself into this situation?* she thought, but I do it all the time. Offering to run the school's art competition as part of local festival day, giving money to the family down the road though if the lady spent less on catalogue goods, they would have a bit more for food. Filling in forms for the illiterate, going to the local Council or Citizens Advice Bureau to try to keep someone from being evicted.

Her mother was always trying to help someone. The neighbours thought she was a soft touch as she would never turn a tramp from the door without a cup of tea and a sandwich. So where does this leave me? she wondered. She thought back to the times when she had tried to win her father's affection, making little gifts for him, a little wooden boat, a drawing or painting. There was always plenty of wood around, Father being a cabinet maker. She was artistic even at a young age. She looked down at the scar on her finger from borrowing her brother's pen knife and carving herself instead of the boat. At least, that provoked a reaction from father. I am a mixture of my mother's good nature and trying to get people to like me. Father was never physically cruel. He just didn't notice that I was there, she thought ruefully.

The only place she was not submissive was at work. She was the boss. She tried always to be fair, but it was difficult. However, the patients always came first and personalities had to be subdued.

Why all this introspection suddenly? Because she had taken on a project too far this time and when this was sorted out, it had to stop.

'I'm tired, kids,' she addressed the cats. 'You can sleep in here tonight. Hot water bottle and bed for me.' She gently pushed Fluff off her lap, turned off the fire, stroked Ivan and headed for the kitchen. By tomorrow morning, the two animals would be curled up close to each other for warmth and friendship.

Having checked that the girl was still sound asleep, she went into her own bedroom. She undressed quickly and got into bed settling on the very edge so as not to lie where Daniel had slept. Exhaustion soon took over and she fell into a deep sleep.

She woke as first light filtered into the room. Wandering across the room she gazed out of the window. The view was stunning. The sky was suffused with streaks of pink, the water in the creek shone like silver showing up the mass of trees along the edge. A couple of fishing boats were heading out to sea, the faint purring of their engines wafting inland.

A noise from the small bedroom brought her back to earth and she looked in to see the girl sitting up in bed, looking around as though she did not know where she was. Her eyes had lost their haunted look though she moved back in the bed still staring when Alexa went in. 'Would you like a cup of tea? Well. I'll bring you one anyway.'

Alexa went downstairs to be greeted by the cats demanding food. 'You can go for a run,' she said unlocking the door. 'Go on. If I feed you first, you'll play me up and not come back for hours. Breakfast will bring you home.'

She made two mugs of tea, putting two spoonsful of sugar in one, carried them upstairs and held the sweetened one out to the girl. Sitting herself on the end of the bed she patiently waited until the girl finally stretched out a hand and took the mug.

Progress, she thought silently.

'I am going to give you a nice hot bath and wash that lovely hair,' pronounced Alexa. 'I have washed your clothes but they are not quite dry so I will lend you some of mine as we have to go into Falmouth to the kind lady who is trying to find you somewhere to stay.' She didn't say *You can't go into town in that peculiar outfit you were wearing yesterday*, even if she thought it.

Having run the bath and checked the temperature, she went upstairs again and with much persuasion and persistence got the girl into her dressing gown and down to the bathroom.

'You must have had a bath at some time. There is nothing to be frightened of. I shan't look at you. I shall turn my back when you take your clothes off.'

The minutes wore on, the clothes landed on the floor, and with a quick splash she was in.

Holding out a bottle of body wash, she poured some onto her hands and motioned to the girl to do the same. After some hesitation, it was accepted.

'Now,' she said, 'rub it on your body,' which looked and smelt as if it needed it. *I wonder when she last had a good wash. Heavens. What a struggle. I don't think I would make a very good nurse.*

Although she dealt with patients all the time at work, she got the interesting bits; asking questions, taking blood, doing tests. I have a new respect for washing them, attending to their wounds, replacing the dressings, tending to them in every way.

Back to the task in hand, she exchanged the bottles for shampoo, squirting a little on the long, but somewhat greasy, grubby hair. Massaging in the shampoo, the girl tried to push her away. Alexa, admiring the coppery blond tresses that kept on appearing, persisted and eventually was rewarded by a mane of beautiful wavy hair gently curling at the ends. After rinsing, she mopped off the excess water with a towel.

Holding up the dressing gown, Alexa enticed the girl to come out of the bath. With another gazelle leap, she dived into the gown and quickly covered herself up. With a clean towel, she started to dry herself off.

Well at least she smells better, thought Alexa. Now about some clothes. She anticipated another battle.

'You can use some of my clothes for today until we get you some new ones. That'll be fun won't it. Do you like shopping?'

She handed the girl a pair of cotton briefs and a sleeveless vest, 'Best I can do. I don't think a bra and bikini pants would be right at this stage,' she surmised. 'Now the skirt,' as she handed over a full length denim version, and ready prepared, pulled in the waist with a couple of safety pins. 'Thank Heavens we are not too different in size.' A striped T-shirt completed the outfit. A bit Orphan Annie, but with thick socks and the girl's own lace-up boots, she looked almost of this era.

'This is like having a baby to look after,' thought Alexa. 'Fancy having to do this every day.'

'Breakfast,' she said, 'toast, cereal, boiled egg?' With no reply she dished out toast and marmalade and another cup of tea.

The cats had returned and had their food. Shying away from the girl they made a beeline for Alexa's bed upstairs and a few more hours rest. 'You animals live the life of Riley,' she shouted up the stairs. *Who was Riley? Not now, not now Alexa.*

After a quick tidy-up, she handed the girl a thick cardigan. 'Put this on. We have to go into Falmouth and get you some help. Won't you tell me your name or where you come from?' Clearly, the girl was overwhelmed by having a bath and being put into strange clothes but at least the wide-eyed look of terror had gone and she was consenting to do as she was asked.

Putting on her own sweater, Alexa called up the stairs. 'Bye kids. See you later.' Talking to the cats again.

Taking the girl's arm, she gently propelled her out of the door towards the car. This time she got in with no protest and allowed the seat belt to be clipped in place. After opening the gates Alexa reversed out, and turning the car, drove her way back along the farm track to the lane and on to Falmouth.

It was still fairly early and plenty of parking space available. The girl got out of the car without being told and went over and leant on the railings overlooking the great expanse of water. Alexa went over and stood next to her. It seemed to attract the girl who stared at it as though she had never seen anything like it. Perhaps she hadn't.

Falmouth, probably the deepest harbour in the world, attracted a wide variety of craft. To the right liners, working ships, grey-painted naval vessels, all anchored in the deepest section were in for repair. Closer to them and spreading out into the bay were the ocean going yachts, elegant luxury vessels with huge sails stowed along the decks. Tied up directly below them small craft were tossing and turning creating bell-like sounds as the chains danced on the incoming tide.

Alexa looked up into the girl's face, seeing for the first-time animation, eyes alight with interest.

'Those great big ships travel across the sea all round the world collecting and delivering goods. The big yachts,' she pointed at the luxury vessels, 'are owned by people who love sailing, who do it for pleasure.' She wasn't sure if the girl was listening, but she carried on talking about the harbour and the ships just in case.

'The water narrows as it flows inland. There is a boatyard up there, pointing inland to the left. Fishermen gather oysters; they are very expensive to buy.' I am yattering like a schoolteacher. *I don't fancy the slimy things slipping down my throat;* Alexa shuddered at the thought.

'Come on,' she said and took the girl's arm. 'Let's go and do some shopping.'

There was no resistance as Alexa led her up into the main shopping area. The girl looked around with lively interest at the selection of shops. Tourist haunts selling clay model mermaids and lighthouses, paintings by local artists mostly of views of the coastline or picturesque villages, food shops, clothes shops—an endless variety.

Conceited of me but I can paint better than some of those, thought Alexa. *Having won a number of local prizes and three paintings in the Mall Gallery, I could probably sell a few.* Holidaymakers as a rule want something to take home as a souvenir, a memory of a lovely time in Cornwall. There was one artist whose work stood out. He was a brilliant young man who painted nautical scenes as easily as making breakfast. He would stand talking to you as he created magical scenes of old sailing ships in a storm or a crabber appearing through the mist. She had a couple of his works at home and hoped to buy some more. At the end of the long and winding street were the two fashion shops; nothing too modern or outrageous.

As the automatic doors swung back, Alexa grasped the girl's arm more firmly and propelled them into the shop and headed for skirts. She selected three and held them up. 'You choose one. It's for you.'

The girl stared a while then selected one in navy and white splashed with poppies. Alexa held it up against her and estimating the size picked out one from the rail. 'Nice, pretty. Now we'll get a t-shirt, plain, nothing extreme.'

At the lingerie section, Alexa picked up a pack of cotton pants. The sort her mother used to wear, brief but practical. This was not the time for bikinis or thongs which seemed to be the norm these days for the youngsters but a definite improvement on those long-legged bloomers the girl had arrived in. Sizing her up, she picked out a bra. That would be another session of explanation and persuasion. Having made and paid for the purchases, 'Dinner,' she announced and made for the pasty shop next door. The girl was walking meekly beside her like a lamb following Mary and didn't appear ready to make a runner. Pasties bought, 'Now we have to go to the Help Trust.'

At the door of the office, the girl hung back and was clearly reluctant to go in.

'You are quite safe. I am here. Don't be afraid,' said Alexa. 'Let's go in and talk to the lady,' who immediately dunked teabags and milk into three mugs adding a couple of sugars to one of them.

Putting them down on the table, she turned to Alexa, 'Has she told you her name yet?'

'No. She hasn't spoken a word but she does seem a lot less scared than she was.'

'Come on, love. What's your name?' asked Irene. Still the girl sat there mute. Irene turned to Alexa. 'I don't know what to do with her. We only have boys in at the moment and I think they would frighten her. The girls' hostels can be pretty rough, some on drugs, pregnant teenagers; it just wouldn't be right. Would you have her for another night until I can sort something out?'

'Well yes,' Alexa heard herself saying as she always did, 'but I am worried about the legality. I don't want to be had up for kidnapping.'

'I trust you and it would be helping this lass. I would always back you up. I'll get on to headquarters and see if they can suggest something.' Turning to the girl, she said, 'I am going to call you Anna. Alright?'

'I must be nuts,' said Alexa as she turned to Irene. 'I'll ring you in the morning before I drive into Falmouth. Let's go, Anna. See what tomorrow brings. This can't go on, Irene.'

'You're a good person. Hear from you tomorrow.'

'Well, that solves a problem for Irene and leaves me with a bigger one,' Alexa muttered to herself.

'Have you seen the sea or a big river before?' she asked Anna, now recently named by Irene. No reply: she assumed not. 'Home. Feed us and the cats.'

Anna got into the car and strapped on the seatbelt. Alexa tried not to show surprise. *She learns very quickly, or she has done it before, and her memory is returning.* She drove off through the town back to the cottage.

In the kitchen, Alexa prepared vegetables and put the pasties in the oven to heat up. She fed the cats and let them out into the garden. Anna sat herself in her chair and stared at the blank screen on the television.

'You have to switch it on.' Alexa did the necessary. The screen lit up, faces appeared, people spoke. Anna watched in fascination.

'Dinner ready.' As she placed the plates on the table. 'Dinner ready,' she called out a bit louder. Anna was becoming a TV addict already.

At the table, Anna picked up a knife and fork, stabbed the pasty and pushed a large piece in to her mouth. With mouth half open, she chewed and gobbled at the food.

My God. She's not used to fine dining, more like hog in trough, was Alexa's thought. *The more I see of this girl, the less I understand. You couldn't take her anywhere. Thank goodness I didn't take her in for a coffee in Falmouth.* She felt herself getting hot under the collar at the thought of it.

Attracting her attention, Alexa cut off a small piece of pasty and with her fork placed it in her mouth, pulled her lips together and quietly chewed.

'Eat quietly,' she said.

After several admonitions, the mouth was closed and the disgusting slurping ceased.

Round one to me.

The ice cream that followed caused another setback. She examined this strange white stuff with suspicion.

'Eat it. It's nice.'

Once tasted, it was shovelled in as though someone else might get it first.

'Slowly, quietly.'

Still on round one, I guess.

'Go on. Back to your television.'

Alexa gathered up the dishes and did the washing up.

The cats came running as she called them and headed through the kitchen into the main room. They and Anna had reached an uneasy truce. No longer actually afraid of her, they settled down on the settee. It was interesting to see that Anna took no notice of them; they were just there and not pets in the way that Alexa, family and friends treated them.

Settled down with a book beside the cats, her mind wondered what she was to do with Anna. The television droned on in the background.

Out of the corner of her eye, her attention was drawn to movement. Anna had turned in her chair and was looking directly at Alexa. It was disconcerting as she gazed straight ahead, eyes wide open. Alexa heard a voice saying, 'My name be Roisin.' Had Anna spoken or was it the television?

The tone was deep with a strong Devon accent. Roisin was quaint, old-fashioned but the girl had spoken. Thinking quickly, she smiled and said, 'What a pretty name. My name is Alexandra though I am always called Alexa. Alexa Moray. Do you have a surname, a family name?'

'My name be Roisin Kelly.'

Desperate to keep her talking without sounding obtrusive, she queried, 'Rosheen. Am I saying it correctly? Such a lovely name.'

'Yes.' She nodded.

'Where do you live? Do you know where you came from?' said Alexa.

'I asked my dad once and he said we came from Down,' said Roisin. 'I said down where, and he said you are silly, so I don't really know.'

Down. County Down in Northern Ireland. That would explain the way she spoke with the words going up an octave at the end of every sentence plus a touch of Devon burr, no doubt picked up from any local people she might have met. Also, Kelly is a very Irish name. 'I have a house near London,' said Alexa. 'My friend Daniel used to come with me, but he died so this is the first time I have come alone.' *Am I talking too much? Give Roisin a chance to say something.*

'It's pretty here. I like the big river that gets bigger and wider.'

'You have not seen a large stretch of water before?'

'I liked the big harbour we saw yesterday. All those boats that travel over the world. How big is the world?'

Alexa ventured hesitantly, 'The world is vast, huge, very big. Where did you go to school?'

'What's school?'

'A place children go to learn.'

'I learned from my dad and Grace.'

'Who is Grace?'

'Grace do live with us. She do the cooking and house cleaning. She do tell me things.'

'Is your mum there?' queried Alexa. She hoped she wasn't treading on delicate ground.

'My dad says my mum died when I was two so I don't remember her. Grace is sort of like my mum but she is old.'

'What have you learned from Grace?'

'I can milk a cow and a goat. I can make jam. I help the men and the boys stook the hay and bring it to the barn for the animals in winter. Grace do teach me my letters and sums, but I am not very good at it.'

Alexa looked across at this fey, attractive young woman. She felt excited. If she could get a little more information, with Philp's help, they might be able to find out where she had come from.

'You live on a farm?'

'What's a farm? I do live in the village.'

'Do you know the name of the village?'

'It don't have no name.'

'Where is it?'

'It be out on the moor.' She paused. 'Down a hill, in the trees.'

'Do you mind my asking lots of questions? We are only trying to help you. To help you find your family again.'

'No. I don't mind but I don't want to go back. I don't want to marry Hugh. He's old and he smells but my dad says I have to.' In fact, Hugh was only about ten years older than Roisin, a handsome man who kept himself clean and smelt only of hay and hedgerows.

Now we are getting somewhere, thought Alexa.

The idea of marrying Roisin off to Hugh was entirely James's attempt to provide a leader for the group and to protect Roisin in the future if anything should happen to him. Hugh, not privy to this, looked on Roisin as a child rather than a future wife. He would have been as horrified as Roisin was.

'Your walk by the river with Hugh. How did it happen?'

Roisin paused and looked straight at Alexa. 'My dad said why don't you go for a walk with Hugh?' and I said, 'no, I don't want to. I want to go with Conor.'

'"You are still young, and Conor is a nice boy but you are both too young to get serious. I have seen you cuddling together. I am getting older, and I want to know that you will be safe. Grace is getting older too. Hugh will look after you".'

'So, you went for a walk by the river with Hugh.'

'Yes.'

'Did Hugh touch you or try to kiss you?'

Roisin looked shocked. 'No.'

'And then you ran away. Let me tell you what I think. Your dad sounds like a lovely caring man. He has lost his parents, his brother and his wife and he doesn't want to lose you or young James. He only wants what is best for you. Talk to him. Tell him that you like Conor and only want to be his friend at present. I am sure he will understand. He must be worried out of his mind about you.'

Roisin who had been looking at the floor suddenly looked up with tears in her eyes. 'I want to go home.'

'And we will try to get you back there. That nice policeman we met in Falmouth, he knows the moor and he is going to help us. Now a few more questions to give us a better idea of where you have come from. How many live in the village?'

'I'm not sure. About four families, some young children.'

'Do you all live together?'

'Oh no,' she cried quite vehemently. 'There's three houses and the barns for the cattle and a smaller one for the horses. They're called Whalebone and Clearway. My dad and Grace and me and my brother young James do live in the biggest one.'

'What wonderful names, the horses. Who named them?'

'My dad. They had two horses on the old home farm when he were a boy. The ones we've got now are small but sturdy. Dad got them at the farmers' market when our old ones died.'

Alexa took a deep breath as she tried to take it in. It was like a rerun of "Lorna Doone", but Philip had said that there were deep areas of the moor where people can hide and get cut off completely from the outside world.

She didn't like to write it down while the girl was talking. *I must try and remember it all; it is quite fascinating.*

'Let's have a cup of tea,' said Alexa; the panacea for all ills.

Alexa carried the mugs into the living room and handed one to Roisin. She must call her that and not Anna any longer.

'Were you running away from Hugh when I first saw you?'

'Yes. I won't marry him. I want to be with Conor.'

'Well, you don't have to. Did you know where you were going?'

'No. I haven't been out of the village, well, only in the fields beyond where the sheep and cattle go or to the plot to plant and look after the vegetables. We got fruit trees and bushes and we do pick blackberries and nuts from the hedges. I did go for a walk with Conor down by the stream but I was frightened my dad might find out.'

'It sounds as though you are self-sufficient then.'

Roisin looked across questioningly. 'I mean,' said Alexa, 'you grow or make everything in or around your compound. You don't go out to the village or the town to buy food?'

'My dad do take sheep or cattle to a market to sell sometimes and he brings back sugar and tea and things like that. And he do buy new animals to keep our herds going.'

'How does he get the cattle to and from the market?'

'Some he puts on a horse and cart and one of the men and a dog do walk behind with the rest.'

'Does Conor go sometimes? Is that how you hear about the outside world?' Alexa paused. 'Do you remember how you got to the road when I first saw you running towards me through the mist?'

'No. not really. I just ran. I remember seeing a house and there was a great big rock above me, and it was dark.'

This might mean something to Philip. *Somehow, we have to get this young woman back to where she had come from though how long this community could survive there with all the technology available to track them down.* Yet Alexa did not want to expose them; they seemed to have survived a long time without being found.

'Off to bed with you,' Alexa said. 'You have had a tiring day. We will talk about it tomorrow.'

She went into the kitchen, put the kettle on, filled a hot water bottle and handed it to Roisin who took it from her and headed towards the stairs.

'Goodnight. Sleep well.'

In only a few days, she had begun to accept the modern world. *She is showing trust in me*, thought Alexa. *Perhaps she is seeing the advantages of the modern world; it should not be difficult for Conor to leave and work as a farmer*, she thought. There were plenty of opportunities available on the managed part of the moor. *Hey. I am matchmaking, getting ahead of myself. Lots of water will flow under the bridge before then.*

She opened up her laptop and started to type all that she had learned from Roisin, sitting there till the early hours of the morning, determined to record it all until fatigue forced her to her bed. Before she finally nodded off, she mused about Roisin's way of speaking, a mixture of old English, a touch of Devon burr and definitely a lot of Irish.

33

Alexa woke after only a few hours' sleep. All the information from Roisin was whirling through her head. What was the Irish connection. How did her father get to England and why? More to the point, how did he end up in Devon with a crowd of followers? He must be a very resourceful man. If Roisin was brought up on the moor, then she would know no other life. Until the village was discovered, it was only supposition.

She crawled out of bed and looked in on Roisin who was still fast asleep. Let her sleep on for a while. She went downstairs, fed the cats, let them out and made herself a cup of tea. Ivan and Fluff had familiarised themselves with the garden and came back when they wished, often bringing a mouse or regrettably a small bird.

The sky was clear with the promise of a fine day ahead. I might take Roisin for a walk along the small beach at the bottom of the garden. She seems fascinated by large open stretches of water. The cats will follow us. They like to chase the insects and small crabs.

Roisin, shocked to find that you had a shower every day, was persuaded to try on a bra. 'Put your arms through the straps and do it up at the back,' commanded Alexa.

Eventually, it was fixed in place; Roisin looked down at herself. 'Pretty,' she said. Another milestone.

After washing the breakfast dishes and making the beds, they walked down the long stretch of grass behind the house onto the narrow beach only visible at low tide. The cats immediately began chasing things and having a high old time as the small waves washed in.

The two girls turned to the right where the creek ended, Roisin collecting shells, pieces of seaweed and coloured stones. On the way, they passed a small mound of rock and for a moment there was a lump in Alexa's throat and tears sprang to her eyes. In former times, when she and Daniel got a view of the mound, they would race to it and the first one there would scramble to the top and cry, 'I am Lord of all I survey.' Stupid, childish game, a mixture of sad and happy memories.

Where the creek narrowed in, rowing boats and small sailing craft were marooned on the thick, deep mud until the tide turned. Some years ago a group came down to the end of the creek in a small motorboat, stayed a bit too long, when the tide turned and they were left stuck on the mud for hours, cold and miserable. You can't argue with the sea. It would have been a major operation to rescue them and as they were in no danger the locals decided to teach them a lesson and leave them there.

Just above the tail of the creek stood an old stone building called The Smoke House. Originally, it had been just that; a place where the pilchards, plentiful and much in demand, were dealt with by the women from the nearby village. It was hard work and left their hands red and raw. Nowadays the house was a luxury holiday home. Alexa, Roisin and the cats prowled round the garden inspecting the channels that ran down to the creek which were used to wash all the fish guts away with the tide. Seagulls would sweep down screaming and flapping their wings and hoover up all the entrails in no time at all.

Were they attracted by the smell? They seemed to have their own mobile phone system, hundreds of them arriving in a great flock. At least, it kept down the smell of rotting fish.

The path wound sharply upwards back to the cottage leaving her out of breath. Cattle followed them along inside the hedge hopeful for food.

After a cup of coffee, Alexa asked Roisin if she would answer some more questions. 'Then we need to contact Philip at the police station to see if he has any news. Your dad and Grace and,' she paused, 'Conor must be really worried about you.'

At this, Roisin began to snivel then really cry. 'Do you want to go home?' asked Alexa.

'I like it here. I like all the new things, but I want to see my folks.'

'Of course, you do. We will get you back as soon as we can as soon as we can find the way. Think hard about anything you saw on the path across the moor. Philip knows the area very well; he might well be able to recognise something. We are all trying help you. You seemed surprised that I expect you to have a bath or shower every day. Are you able to have a bath at home?'

'Yes, the men get buckets of water from the pump and heat it up over a fire then everyone gets cleaned up and has their clothes washed.'

'What about every day?'

'We wash our hands and face at the pump.' So that explained the rather unsanitary smell of Roisin.

'The men dug a well and made the pump. So my dad said but we wash in the stream in the summer; it runs outside the village alongside the field where the cattle and sheep do live so they can drink from it.'

Alexa was beginning to build a picture of village life. A collection of houses in a deep, hidden valley with adjacent grazing land for cattle and sheep and an area to grow corn and vegetables, a well, a water pump. Yes. They were self-sufficient. Amazing that they had not been discovered before now. You read about it in books, but it was still happening in the twenty first century. She recalled reading a book entitled "Earth to Earth" about a Devon family, two brothers and a sister, who had got cut off from the outside world and were still using Victorian machinery and cutting all the hedges by hand in the 1950s. It had ended in tragedy when they got too old to cope any longer and could not face the modern world. One brother killed the other two and then himself committed suicide. She had read this book many times, fascinated how such a situation was possible in this day and age and here it was happening again.

She had exposed a world apart and she doubted if the local villagers would be very happy about it although the group caused no harm. *We shall have to make up a believable story for Roisin before she returns.*

'We had better go in and talk to Philip; he may have found out a little more,' she said.

The evening was spent with Roisin glued to the television while Alexa walked up a nearby hill to get a signal on her mobile arranging to visit Philip at the police station.

He was fascinated to hear what Alexa had learned and said he would get out his ordnance survey map of the moor and see if he could work out the route back to the "village". They arranged to meet at ten o'clock the next day.

'If we do find it, will you feel duty-bound to report it to the authorities?' asked Alexa.

'A difficult question. Let's discuss it tomorrow.' She bade him goodnight and returned to the cottage, surprised to find the cats had followed her. 'Come on kids. Home.'

The next morning, cats safely shut in, they set off for what might be Roisin's last trip to Falmouth. She almost leapt out of the car and ran to gaze out at the bay and the ships.

Philip was waiting for them at the police station. With a large Ordinance Survey map laid out on his desk. 'Lisa,' he turned to a young woman in police uniform, 'will you look after Roisin for a bit? Cup of tea and there's a couple of fashion magazines she might like to look at. We'll be in the interview room.'

'Yes Sarge. What if any customers come in?'

'Well deal with them. What does she think she's paid for?' he muttered. Philip laid out the map. 'Has she said anymore?'

'She has got a bit more talkative and remembers seeing a house below her because it had a light on and running alongside a wall of stone way above her.'

'See here,' pointing at the map. 'That could well be at the north end of the moor in the direction of the A30. There is a walkers' path; she might have followed that. It is not much used as you get noise from the firing range. But it doesn't tell us where she started from.'

'She likes all the modern things but says she wants to go back.'

'Why don't we go to the moor starting at the place you first saw her and follow the walkers' path to the northern end? I think I know what the tall stone rock above her might be and you can see a farmhouse down in a shallow valley. I can go tomorrow if you can get ready in time.'

'Philip.' Alexa looked at him worriedly. 'I can't expect you to give up a day off.'

'I'll book it in as official. They can do without me for a day. I haven't been up that way for some years; it will be a day out for me.'

'You won't wear police uniform, will you? It might frighten her.'

'No, no, my lover. I'll dig out my walking togs. Park your car in the police station car park here. That will save you a large parking fee. We'll take my car. I can claim for the petrol.'

'That's kind of you. What time would suit you?'

'About nine-thirty; it's quite a drive up there.'

'Right then. See you tomorrow. Thank you for your help and interest, Philip. I do appreciate it.' She glanced at this kindly, genial man. 'I think you are enjoying it,' she said.

'You're welcome. I couldn't bear the thought of that girl being put in a hostel and it will be a change from dealing with petty thieves and drug addicts.'

'Now we have to get you another bra,' said Alexa as they emerged from the police station. 'You can choose the colour.'

The first one had fitted well. 'Good guess on my part,' as they crossed to the underwear department and found a similar size and style. 'You choose what colour you want.' After much deliberation, a bright pink was selected and paid for.

'You do know we are going to try and find your home tomorrow, don't you? So you had better take a last look at the bay and the ships.'

Back at the cottage, after pasty and tea they settled down with the cats. *We seem to be living on pasties, but they are quick and easy to serve up and I don't know what else she eats. Ice cream was almost a touch too far.*

'I want to ask a few more questions. OK?' Roisin nodded. 'What are the houses made of?'

Roisin considered for a moment. 'Some of them are made of rocks sort of piled on top of one another and some from trees with mud filling up the holes and they all have roofs of straw. Each man made his own beds and tables and things. After we have gathered the wheat in, the roofs have more straw put on to keep us warm in the winter.'

'We had better get you packed for tomorrow. You can have my old rucksack. Pack your new clothes and wear the ones you came in.'

'I am not wearing those bloomers,' shouted Roisin.

Alexa laughed. 'No. I take your point there but your dad and Grace might be a bit surprised.'

Roisin looked shocked. 'My dad wouldn't see me in my underthings. Grace might get upset though.'

'They will both be glad to have you back, I'm sure,' replied Alexa. She paused for a minute. 'Now we have to concoct a story that won't upset your dad. We had better say you got upset and ran out of the village and lost your way. Some people looked after you.' Staring directly into Roisin's face, Alexa said, 'Now listen carefully.' Roisin started to cry. 'Your dad will be so pleased to have you back he won't be angry with you. I promise you.'

'These people who looked after you helped you find your way back, but they have not seen the village or know where it is, which is true. You don't want to upset your dad and the others who live there. I hope you will all have many more years of happiness there.'

In her heart, she thought they would not have too many years before they were discovered. *Sad*, she thought. *They are not doing anyone harm. So, what if they don't pay Council tax and water rates. I don't care. Wish them luck.*

She once more concentrated on Roisin. 'I am going to give you a stamped, addressed letter to Philip, the policeman. You must keep it hidden but if you need to escape again, give it to Conor to post when he goes into the cattle market. Now let's go and pack your things; we have to get going quite early.'

Looking into the girl's rather beautiful, innocent face thinking she could be a model in today's world, without the bloomers. 'I shall miss you, Roisin. I hope we meet again someday.'

Roisin looked quite tearful. 'I have never had a friend before. Thank you. I have seen the modern world, but I must return.'

'Will you miss the cats? They seem to like you.'

'Yes. We only have dogs, and they are not very friendly.'

Alexa and Roisin went upstairs, packed their belongings and retired to bed.

Chapter 3

Early next morning, dressed in the clothes she had arrived in, but with modern bra and pants. Roisin came downstairs looking miserable. 'Hey,' said Alexa. 'Cheer up. You are going home today. Hopefully we can find the way back. Here's your breakfast,' as she placed two eggs on toast in front of Roisin with a mug of tea. 'I'll pack a flask and some sandwiches; it is going to be a long day. I am just going next door to see Jen. Shan't be long. You get your things together.'

'Come in.' Jen opened the door. 'What's happening?'

'Well,' replied Alexa. 'Eventually, she started talking and apparently lives in a hidden village in a combe on the moor. It seems they have been there for years. She ran away from her father but now wants to go back. Philip, that nice policeman from Falmouth, used to work up that way and knows the moor quite well is helping us. He has been poring over maps and he thinks he has an idea of where she came from so we are going to try and find this hidden combe.'

'Good luck. Do let me know how you got on. Take care; they might get nasty with intruders.'

'Not if we are returning the girl.'

'Well. I hope not.'

'I am glad she wants to go home,' said Alexa looking up at Jen. 'The authorities would put her in a hostel, and she is not used to being confined. I am sure she would be very unhappy and only run away again.'

'I agree with you,' replied Jen. 'You're a good soul to try and help her.'

'I'm a mug. Got it from my mother. She used to feed all the tramps. They knew they would always get something to eat and a cup of tea if they knocked at the door. Well. Must get on. Wish me luck.'

'I do. Let me know how it goes.'

Back at the cottage, Alexa washed up the breakfast dishes, checked on the cats and called to Roisin who was sitting staring at an empty television screen.

'Come on then. Pick up your rucksack; it's time to go.'

Alexa locked the cottage door and got into the car. Roisin paused to look at the view where the creek widened out to become the sea. It was a clear morning with the sun glinting on the water, catching the tops of the trees that grew up the sides of the inlet. At dawn, the water was a sheet of silver, the sky a rosy pink, the confining trees pale mauve just appearing through the mist. She watched Roisin keenly, hoping she would keep the memory of her time here. Once in the passenger seat of the car Roisin put on her seatbelt without being asked.

There is probably a quicker route to the A39 but Alexa chose to start at the bottom of the town and drive slowly up Killigrew Street so as to give Roisin her final view of the harbour. As traffic always moved at a snail's pace, there was ample opportunity to meander with no horns hooting or shouting from irate drivers. Roisin turned herself sideways almost leaning on Alexa and gazed at the great expanse of water with small boats bobbing on the tide, their jangling chains playing a tune. Further in the distance were the warships and huge cargo ships. Pointing in that direction, Roisin said, 'Those big boats. They are the ones that go to the world, aren't they?'

'Well. The world is made up of lots of different countries. We are in England at the moment. So yes, the big boats go all over the world, to places like Africa or Australia.'

'Oh,' she replied as though she had not grasped that concept and promptly turned round and stared ahead.

'We had better move on. Philip will be waiting,' said Alexa.

At the top end of the town, she picked up the A39 to the police station, turned in and parked. Philip was standing by his car wearing brown cords, a green anorak and stout walking boots looking every bit a Dartmoor ranger.

'Good morning you two. You in the back, Roisin,' pointing to his car. 'You next to me,' to Alexa. 'You are the one who knows where we are going.'

'The start of where we are going,' she replied. 'I can get you to the layby and then we need your help and knowledge of the moor.'

'I spent quite a bit of time on the moor.' Philip looked quite wistful for a moment, probably wishing he still worked there rather than dealing with drunks and druggies in Falmouth. 'We were mostly looking for lost ramblers but a couple of times hunting down escaped prisoners. They led us a merry dance I can tell you.'

'Did you catch them?'

'We did actually; cold, wet, miserable, hungry. Prison was probably more comfortable.'

'They were a long way from the prison, weren't they?'

'Dartmoor is a huge area. I suppose they thought they could hide here, but the moor can be a cruel, merciless place. This is Carland Cross. We can pick up the A30 interchange here.'

On a rise above the roundabout, a collection of wind turbines were whirring away.

'A lot of people don't like them. I find them attractive,' announced Alexa. 'Better than a conventional power station.'

'Like giants waving their arms,' came a voice from the back seat.

'You are right, Roisin. How poetic.'

Philip negotiated the roundabout and a few miles further on announced, 'Right Alexa, we are getting near to Okehampton; you had better start looking for your layby on the down road.'

Well, it's not going to be on this side, is it? Thought Alexa. *Oh don't be crabby; it's just nerves,* as she turned her head hoping desperately she would recognise the spot. 'That's it.' She pointed across the motorway.

'You're sure?'

'Yes.'

'I shall have to drive to the next roundabout so I can turn back on to the westward road.'

Philip pulled into the layby. A long stretch of grassland led up to a belt of trees. This was the start of the moor. He got out of the car and put official looking police signs on it. 'That should keep it safe for a while. Stop the yobs trying to pinch it.'

Meanwhile, Alexa and Roisin had got out of the car. Alexa was staring across at the expanse of rough grassland leading up to the trees in the distance.

'Do you remember this, Roisin?' The girl shook her head looking confused. 'I don't suppose you do. There was a heavy mist and the rain was chucking it down.'

'Get your rucksacks and we'll try to work it out. You say she came out of the mist. At about what angle?' queried Philip. He was no longer the kindly man listening to the story, handing out cups of tea. Here, in its place, was a sharp, efficient police officer in charge of a difficult situation that needed to be solved. Alexa was impressed.

'Diagonally.' Alexa pondered the problem for a moment. 'Let me see. Straight ahead would be ninety degrees so about 35 to 40 degrees to my right as she pointed to the trees across the grassy area some distance away.'

'OK. You walk in that direction. Roisin, you next and I'll bring up the rear,' said Philip. He was not taking any chance that the girl might make a run for it.

Alexa strode off and stopped at the line of trees; thin hazel saplings, an occasional spiky blackthorn with its profusion of tiny white flowers which would later yield the sloes so beloved of gin drinkers. It was a barrier but not an impenetrable one. If Roisin had broken through in this direction with a bit of effort, they could find a gap and break in on to the path.

'There seems to be a small gap here,' said Philip. 'She must have come through that and continued on down on a natural curve to the road. I doubt she would have come from the left as she would have had to make a ninety-degree turn.' He pushed through the trees and bushes on to a narrow, somewhat overgrown path. 'Come on; we'll try this way.'

Alexa pushed Roisin in through the gap and followed to take her place in the line-up.

Philip strode off with the girls behind him not that Roisin could escape as the path was too hemmed in by the enclosing foliage. Outside it had been bright with sunshine and flowers. Here in the wood, it seemed to Alexa to be dark and confined, overpowering.

She tended to be a bit claustrophobic, panicked if a lift stopped between floors. She found herself breathing quickly and longed to get back into the open air but she had promised Roisin she would get her home, so she had to do her best.

The trees were now closer together on the other side of the path and except for an occasional bird tweet the place was eerily silent. They trudged on until Philip called a halt at an even narrower path which branched off to the left sloping uphill and deeper into the wood.

'I am pretty certain she would not have come down that path,' said Philip, consulting his ordnance survey map. 'That leads up to Stannon Tor which is a very large open area with two prehistoric standing stone circles. There would be absolutely nowhere you could hide one house let alone three or four. We had better keep going along this one.'

He folded up his map and they set off again.

Some way further along, a tree had fallen by the wayside. Alexa feeling hot and exhausted, called out, 'Let's have a rest' and, plonking herself down on a protruding branch, opened up her rucksack and handed round plastic mugs of coffee from her flask. 'Have a sandwich,' and held out the plastic box.

They all sat munching when Philip stood up and called out, 'Come on. We must keep going.'

Following what seemed to Alexa like another mile, the path took a long wide curve upwards. Philip halted, pulled out his map and looked at it.

'I don't think it would be up there. That goes up to the firing range. Much too noisy and dangerous. Hey up. There is something going on here.'

Roisin had stopped in her tracks, her feet dancing up and down and was staring at the scrubby bushes to the right of the path backed by closely packed, seemingly impenetrable holly and blackthorn.

The girl seemed terribly agitated, waving her arms and almost dancing on the spot.

'Do you recognise this?' said Alexa taking her by the arm.

The girl continued to look extremely upset then turned and almost wrapped herself around Alexa in a tight bearhug. She suddenly let go and dashed across to the bushes and disappeared from sight.

Confused by what was happening, Philip stood stunned for a few seconds, then thrust himself at the place where Roisin had gone followed closely by Alexa. The bushes were not as impenetrable as they had seemed and apart from a few scratches from the blackthorn they arrived in an area of woodland. They stood stock still. The place was eerily silent. Both were startled when an animal, probably a rabbit, ran across ahead of them kicking dried leaves up in the air, creating a small brown snowstorm. Looking ahead they could see a trail where Roisin had run, but there was no sign of her. She had just disappeared.

The area had a feeling of age about it as though no one had disturbed it for centuries. The trees were very tall with huge, gnarled trunks partly covered in moss. The canopy of leaves above shut out most of the light. Tall thin saplings struggled upwards in an attempt to survive. A few small patches of sunlight slanted down creating intermittent patterns on the forest floor. As they became more accustomed to the gloom and the silence, a faint gurgling and splashing came to their ears.

'There must a stream down there in the valley,' said Philip.

'I recall Roisin telling me she and Conor walked along by a river when they could escape from James for a while. Shall we try to follow her?'

'No,' replied Philip curtly. 'I am sure she will find her way home; she seemed to know where she was going. We might not get a very nice welcome. I think the village will be discovered before too long and what I haven't seen I can't report.'

They pushed their way back through the bushes and started their long homeward trek, Philip leading the way. Alexa felt the enclosed feeling coming over her again and longed to get out of the place. After what seemed hours, Philip called out, 'Here we are.' Sunlight shed a ray across the path exposing the gap out on the grassland. Alexa pushed her way through and took deep gulps of fresh air. Looking down they could see the car below them and made their way down towards it.

'Any coffee left?'

Alexa shook the flask. 'Enough to revive us,' and poured out the remains and handed a mug to Philip.

'Well. That was an adventure,' he said between slurps.

'One I would rather not repeat. It was creepy in there. I hope she will be alright.'

'Don't worry. I am quite certain she will. She obviously recognised the place and knew where she was going. Your work is done.'

On the way back to Falmouth, Philip was quiet then said suddenly, 'I know that place. I remember it now, but our team approached it from the other side. We were looking for a pair of lost ramblers. There are the remains of quarry workings approached by a gentle slope and over to the right a thick belt of trees. It would be an ideal place to hide and with a piece of open land above the quarry again surrounded by trees for their horses and livestock, ideal for their needs. The quarry hasn't been in use for nearly a hundred years. Very few people visit that wild part of the moor, not even the rangers. I reckon that is where they will be. Good luck to them. They haven't caused any trouble and James has found sanctuary for his family and followers. I vote we just leave them to live their lives until...' he paused, '...they are dragged into the modern world.'

Philip had reverted from the efficient policeman to the kindly man.

Outside the police station, they got out of the car. Alexa put her arms around Philip. 'I cannot thank you enough.'

'You are welcome, my love.'

'Let me know if you hear anything,' she said looking up into his face.

He nodded and smiled. Alexa got into her car and drove off back to the cottage, back to the cats to begin her holiday.

'Did you find the ramblers?' asked the young policewoman back at the station.

'Yes. Wet, cold, tearful. They will learn to read a map before they visit the moor again. It's a tricky old place,' replied Philip.

Chapter 4

Sitting in the living room with the cats beside her on the settee, Alexa could not dismiss the whole episode of Roisin from her mind. What was the history of James Kelly? What had made him abandon his smallholding, his country, to try his luck in England?

Life must have been desperate to have driven him to take such a decision. I must delve into the history of Ireland to see if that explains it. I know that millions of the population migrated to America and other countries during and following the Great Potato Famine. Perhaps the poverty carried on down the generations. Also I should like to know more of Dartmoor, that great mysterious tract of land with its hidden combes, prehistoric circles, legends of ancient peoples and fearsome animals like the Hound of the Baskervilles. Meanwhile I shall do some painting, take long walks by the sea, eat fresh fish and relax.

She went upstairs hoping for a good night's sleep. It was only four or five days since she had set out for Cornwall; it seemed like a lifetime.

Alexa got up late, took the cats for a walk, came back and got out her paints. She tried painting the view of the creek but felt she had not done it justice. Such a beautiful place; it deserved better than that. Try again another day.

Her mind kept reverting to the events of the past few days and the reason James Kelly had led his folk on to the moor. *I'll go into Falmouth library this afternoon and see what they have got on the Irish Potato Famine. There is more to the story of James Kelly than I know.* Her habit of finding out things was driving her. *You are not at work now, give it a rest,* but she knew that she would not leave the subject alone until her curiosity was satisfied.

In Falmouth, she found a couple of books to start on. Whatever she was writing, medical or otherwise, she always went back to basics. Get the broad outline first then home in on to the detail. Feeling the need for a scone and thick Cornish cream she indulged herself in the café overlooking the harbour. Finding a window seat, she sat watching the boats going past. Always something to catch the eye, something to remind her of Roisin.

Back at the cottage she and the cats made themselves comfortable on the settee and Alexa opened her book. "The Great Hunger" by Cecil Woodham Smith.

James Kelly's (the one now living on Dartmoor) problems of hardship and poverty had commenced over a century ago, travelling down the years, each generation inheriting the misfortunes of their parents until life became untenable and emigration to England seemed the only possible hope of survival.

Back in the 1840s, John James Kelly, the tenant farmer of a smallholding made up of three small plots of land, was producing just enough to feed his growing family and a bit over to take to market The early green crops made the best prices which brought in a little money but did not contribute much to the health of the family. John James would load up his cart with anything saleable, harness up one of the old horses and set off for the nearest town to sell his produce. John James, who was fond of a drink, made it his habit to stop at the public house on the way home considerably reducing any profit he had made at the market.

The main crop and staple diet of the peasantry was potatoes supplemented by buttermilk from the cow and a small amount of pork whenever a pig had been slaughtered. Portions of the animal were salted down to see them through the winter. An occasional luxury was a chicken which had grown old and no longer regularly produced eggs. The carcass stripped of its feathers, would be hacked up and added to the cauldron which permanently sat stewing above the peat fire in the main room of the old homestead. The feathers were stuffed in to sacks to make foul-smelling pillows. Meanwhile, his wife would be milking the cow and tending to the plants growing near to the house and looking after the ever-increasing brood of children.

Collecting the eggs was a job for the children though they rarely got to eat them, most of them going to market to make a few pennies. The family increased with monotonous regularity as James had his wicked way when he returned half-drunk from the market. An Irish wife in those days was almost permanently pregnant and worn down with the worry of how to feed the existing children.

Alexa's holiday came to an end and she returned to work. Years passed and besides the daily routine of the laboratory, there were experiments to plan and increasingly, trips around the country to read a paper at a conference or to update on the recent findings in the world of haemostasis.

She never forgot Roisin and that brief interlude where a girl from the past came into her life. Sometimes it seemed like a dream. Did it really happen? From time to time, she searched the Internet for news that James Kelly and his followers had been discovered. No word came from Philip who had promised to let her know of any developments, so she had to assume that they were safe. So perhaps they should be paying rent and taxes but good luck to them; they deserved a life.

She was called in to the Prof's office one morning to be greeted with, 'I should like you to go to the Gambia to collect lifestyle details and to take blood samples from the native population. You will have to take everything you need. The Gambia has a very low rate of heart disease and we need to find out why.'

In particular, Scotland and Finland who had the highest known rate of heart disease in the world. Details of Russia and China being difficult to obtain. Perhaps it was something to do with their diet, she thought facetiously. Fish, peanuts and okra versus beefburgers, crisps and chips for a start. Though that didn't make sense. Finland with one of the highest rates of heart disease in the world ate sensibly though they had a serious national drink problem put down to three months or more of total darkness when the sun never shone and the inhabitants had to stay indoors with nothing better to do but soak up alcohol.

'Including a liquid nitrogen tank?' she queried tremulously, coming back to the present and the Prof's droning voice. 'We shall need to keep the samples at around minus 180 degrees.' *Oh God. I am not too sure where the Gambia is.* Desperately thinking back to school geography lessons, she had a vague idea that it was on the west coast, on that big bulge of Africa near Senegal.

Interview over, she made a beeline for the library, to discover the Gambia was a thin, narrow country heading inland along the river of the same name. Beyond that, she knew nothing about the place. *I guess I had better do some homework*, she thought.

'Yes, yes. Get it sorted and be ready to go in two weeks,' he had droned on. He had a dreary sort of voice that made you want to go to sleep in the middle of his lecture. Alexa jerked herself back to the present day. The Prof continued, 'The lab accommodation will be available at this time of year.' She began to imagine difficult conversations with the airline.

This seemingly minor task of going to the Gambia accomplished, Alexa found herself the following year in northern Finland up on the Russian border to again bring back samples from a population with, at that time, the highest rate of heart disease in the world. Scotland shared the honours and would be visited later.

She stepped out of Helsinki airport to be met by incredibly freezing weather and a wind coming in from the Arctic that seemed to go in the front of her body, take a shortcut and come straight out through the back. She had never experienced anything like it.

Although it was terribly hard work, there were short periods in both trips when she able to sit back and watch the sunny or snowbound world go by and remember Roisin.

What had happened to her? She wondered. Did she find her way back home? Was she still down in the combe hidden away from the world? The nagging worries lingered on.

The contrasts between the Gambia and northern Finland were extreme. In an upcountry African village, she sat watching the children play. The village was one of the more affluent; hardly the right word, than many in such that they had a basic diet though most of them were riddled with worms and were carriers of Hepatitis from drinking water from a contaminated well or diseases to which they had little resistance.

But they were alive and surviving unlike the Irish peasants who had died in their millions.

In Finland, the children were wrapped up warmly, well fed and went to school. The health problems of their parents were exacerbated by the consumption of large amounts of fat from the animals who had to be kept in the homestead during the devastatingly cold winters. Cut off from the rest of the country by lack of roads there was no alternative. In the two opposing countries Alexa visited, health was a priority and being dealt with at government level. Roads now led up to the north of the country; Health Centres were being built.

Frequently the enigma of James Kelly and his followers came into her mind. The more she read, the more of what she was able to trace back about the family Kelly (God bless the Internet), the more she became convinced that the real problems started with the Potato Famine. There were thousands of Kellys in Northern Ireland but eventually with the help of church records of births and deaths she narrowed the family down to the village of Ballycona in County Down.

The Irish had, for many hundreds of years, been a problem for the British parliament who considered them quarrelsome and uneducated.

The difficulties went far deeper. The Act of Union between Great Britain and Ireland which had given the English landlords dominance over the tenant farmers was a source of hatred by the Irish and was eventually repealed in 1843 after a long struggle led by Daniel O'Donnell. It was hailed as a victory. Ireland was now a separate country. The Irish celebrated. There would be free trade between the two countries. One hundred Irish members sat in the Westminster parliament. Ireland would be better off, in charge of their own affairs. But this was not to be.

Virtually the whole country consisted of farming; it was estimated that ninety three percent of tenants were paying rent to landowners.

Land being scarce and difficult to procure meant that the rents were greatly increased, putting the cost beyond the majority of the tenant farmers. Some were left with no land at all or a plot too small to support the family or not having any crops to sell at market. Either way it ended in hunger and starvation. Even prior to the Potato Famine it was estimated that 2.5 million of the Irish people were starving. Outside of the towns housing of any sort was a luxury. A large number lived in windowless cabins stuck together with mud or in holes in the ground. Furniture of the traditional sort was not an option, parents and children huddling together for warmth under mouldy sacking or with the luckless pig who would eventually be killed and eaten.

Up until the beginning of the 1840s, James John Kelly felt himself a fortunate if discontented man. Now late middle-aged with a docile, hardworking wife and an annual addition to the family, life should be more than having enough to keep everyone fed, a peat fire and beds for the numerous children James was more prosperous than most. They, now the elderly parents, John James and his wife sat in front of the fire, sleeping the day away leaving the James of the next generation to manage the farm. A cow in the yard and free range chickens meant that food was available if not exactly cordon bleu.

James senior married a good woman and they started on their own brood.

Samuel, his brother with a family of his own, was a great friend and the two men shared their problems and helped each other when they could.

Kelly Farmhouse

A little bit of pleasure would not come amiss thought James but life was tolerable. He was a staunch Protestant and attended church on a Sunday to give thanks for what he had. But God did not seem to be in a good mood this year and before too long James would be begging Him for mercy, not praising Him for his goodness.

So one morning with the sun shining, James, son of old James drove the horse and cart down to his allotted acres. The potato tops looked strong and green; the crop would be good this year. The children would be fed and there would be profits to come from selling seed potatoes in the market.

He got out his fork and dug the first tubers. They were large and smooth skinned.

He dug all day leaving them to dry off on the warm soil. Apart from a brief stop for a hunk of bread and a drink of water he worked until the sun got lower in the sky. Putting aside the spade he gave the old horse the remaining water and started to load up the potatoes.

The children ran to meet him screaming and shouting with excitement as he approached the cottage.

'Go and get the sacks from the barn,' he shouted. The kids came running back.

'The tatties are dry enough. We'll get them packed away tonight he thought and take them up to the loft tomorrow. The rest can go in the soil pit to be dug out later in the year.'

Having unharnessed the horse, fed and watered him, James went back to the children. He opened a sack and grabbed a handful of potatoes. He was still pleased and relieved at the fine crop. A few skins slid away and the underlying flesh was soft and slimy. 'Oh damn,' he muttered. 'Sorry Lord. There are a few rotten ones in here. Empty the sacks,' he shouted to the kids, 'and I'll have a look at them. We have to pick out the nasty ones.'

Going over to the emptied sacks, James saw that all of the potatoes lying on the ground had split showing slimy, rotten flesh.

'Oh my God,' he said.

He felt sick; his legs felt as though they were giving way. There had been good years and bad years, but he had never seen anything like this.

'Go to your mother,' he said to the children. 'Tell her I am going over to talk to Samuel.'

The bewildered kids ran towards the cottage wondering why they were being sent indoors. Why was Father angry? They only wanted to help. 'Wash your hands under the pump before you go in,' he called out.

James set off for the long walk to Samuel's homestead. He was close to his younger brother; they looked out for one another, having been through the good and bad times together, giving what little they had and taking from each other when they were able to help. As he walked over the fields he felt cold and empty inside. How would he feed the children? There was virtually no cash in hand. They lived hand to mouth, surviving rather than living.

Samuel stopped sweeping the yard and leaning on his broom called out, 'Hello. What are you doing here at this time of day? I thought you would be out in the fields. Is something wrong, James?' He looked at his brother's pale, pinched face.

'Have you started getting in your potatoes yet?'

'No. I was planning to start next week.'

'Will we walk over and take a look at them?'

'You are worrying me now. What's wrong?'

'Maybe nothing. Let's go and see.'

With James forging ahead, they made their way over to Samuel's allotted land.

'Hang on. I am out of breath. What's the hurry?'

'The light is beginning to fade and I want to get there while we can still see.'

'Well, here we are. What now?' gasped a breathless Samuel.

James inspected a root of potatoes and found a few dead leaves.

'Frost,' said Samuel.

'Put your hands in the soil and pull out a whole root.'

Samuel did as he was told and unearthed a number of good-sized, healthy-looking tubers still clinging to a green stalk.

'Push your fingers through the skin,' commanded James.

A stinking mass of rotten brown flesh was exposed. The stench was unbelievable.

'Pull another one from a different row.' James did as he was told.

The result was the same.

'What's happening?' demanded a bewildered Samuel.

'I don't know but the whole of my crop is the same. In a day, the whole area is dead.'

'The children. What will we feed them on?'

The brothers stared at one another in horror.

'Come on home,' said James. 'There is nothing more we can do here.'

Potato blight

Before long, the whole of Ireland's green fields was turned into a blackened wasteland. People were beginning to starve. Worse was to come.

In July 1845, Robert Peel the Prime Minister received a letter from the Isle of Wight informing him that blight had affected their crops and was already spreading to Kent and the south of England. The low countries on the Continent had a similar problem.

This letter was the first indication that the blight had been brought over on the ships from America. Inevitably the scourge had spread to Ireland who were in no position to withstand its effects. With potatoes being the staple food hunger and disease soon stalked the land.

In 1851, the Census of Ireland reported that there had been twenty-four major crop failures since the 1700s so yet another one was not taken too seriously. Dry rot, Curl and early frost were put down by the scientists of the day as the probable cause.

Ireland would get over it; they had before. They were always moaning about something, the government said.

A number of preposterous proposals were put forward by the government to solve the problem.

The peasants were advised to rasp the diseased potato, wash the pulp and dry it on a griddle.

The starch in the washing liquid could be combined with flour or oatmeal and then baked as bread. Brilliant suggestion. Had no one told the government that the peasants were too weak to follow the instructions and had no money to purchase flour or oatmeal.

The starch was fed to the cattle, who died. More and more of the population succumbed. The government was forced to act.

In 1815, the Corn Laws had been enacted. A massive tax on imported, cheaper grain from foreign countries was imposed ensuring that the farmers were forced to buy from Britain keeping prices high for the greedy landowners. Meanwhile, the peasant farmers suffered.

The Irish had got around the problem of hunger by making potatoes the staple food and selling the excess as seed in the markets.

Robert Peel had been considering this problem for some years and in 1846, the repeal of the Corn Laws got through parliament in an attempt to alleviate the massive problem in Ireland.

This provoked such violent anger by politicians and landowners that Ireland and its starving people became subsumed and almost a secondary issue.

Meanwhile, millions were dying of starvation. Yet as decreed by law, corn, meat and dairy produce was still being exported to England from Ireland. Terrible stories were being told. A soldier on a route march down to the south of Ireland reported blackened fields, total annihilation. People were dying before their eyes. A woman was seen gnawing on stolen raw turnips her children screaming for food. Piles of bodies lay around.

Money was made available by Robert Peel for projects such as road laying and setting up new works. Half of the money would be given as a grant, the other half as a loan to be repaid. But how? The peasants were too weak to carry out the work, so the scheme failed.

The winter of 1846 to 1847 was the longest and harshest in living memory in Ireland with heavy frost, a bitterly cold wind and relentless rain.

Relief groups were set up in London, Dublin and even as far as India but it was too little too late.

To their credit a few, a very few philanthropic landowners gave grain to their tenants in an attempt to replace corn for the staple food, potatoes, but it was not enough.

As the situation deteriorated many decided to emigrate, scraping together their last few pounds and shillings together for the passage. America and Britain being the main goals.

This, of course, led to unscrupulous men cashing in on the situation. "Package brokers", who colluded with ship owners to take a fixed number of emigrants on board ship. The ships going to British North America to collect timber to bring back to Europe were going out empty of cargo so why not fill them with desperate people trying to escape famine in Ireland? A small group of men started up businesses and guaranteed to supply ships with emigrants. A small amount of money for the ship owners was better than none.

The cost of providing bunks below decks was minimal. Each passenger was supplied on the official ships with seven pounds of food per week per passenger. The more honest captains administered the food in small amounts otherwise the whole amount would be eaten at one go. The less honest distributed none. The rations were scarcely enough to keep a rat alive of which there were as many on board as humans.

The conditions were appalling. Seasickness, disease and again starvation ensured that many died, and the bodies thrown overboard. Those who arrived in the promised land were in a pitiful state having brought their diseases with them.

Arriving in Canada, some were canny enough to cross the border and get into America where the population was higher and there was more chance of housing and work.

It was estimated that one million people died of starvation and up to one and a half million emigrated.

Chapter 5

The cause of the potato blight was poorly understood at the time of the famine and scientists declared it was due to a fungus. Further work in the twentieth century found that an oomycete (an algae (lower fungus)-like eukaryote) was responsible; it was designated US-1. Due to the unavailability of scientific methods, it was not possible to identify the particular strain in the 1840s.

In the twenty-first century, a group of international scientists were allowed access to Irish potato leaves which had been stored at Kew Gardens since 1847. By modern DNA sequencing, they found a previously unknown strain which they called HERB-1 and considered that this was the cause of potato blight responsible for the Irish famine.

US-1 had been previously cited as the cause of the worldwide infection until the HERB-1 variant was identified.

The wild potato Solanum tuberosum is indigenous to the Toluca valley in Mexico. Somehow it migrated to the slopes of the Andes and was consumed by the population at least ten thousand years ago. From there, it was possibly transported by the ships to America and Europe, particularly Ireland. In his review article, Joseph Stromberg suggests that the two strains of Phytophthora infestants split soon after their common ancestor made it out of Mexico. Other authors feel that the divergence came much later. The strain HERB-1 responsible for the famine, appeared to die out around one hundred and fifty years ago and probably does not exist today. The strain US-1 is still surviving in various parts of the world and causing considerable potato damage.

Chapter 6

Life for Alexa had slowed down. She attended a number of meetings in the UK but with no trips abroad she was able at weekends to visit libraries, the National Newspaper collection and of course the Internet to look into the cause and effect of the Potato Famine in Ireland and in particular how it had affected James Kelly's family down the generations. In particular, why had James Kelly, in the 1950s, finally abandoned his few acres in Ballycona in the hope of finding a better life in England?

Alexa still managed to get down to the cottage in Cornwall twice a year taking the cats.

There she managed a little peace and quiet sitting on the patio, just gazing at that incredible view and walking the cats along the beach.

It was when she drew the curtains and got out all the research papers she had gathered that the utterly appalling facts of the Irish Potato Famine overcame her, depressed her, oppressed her. It was such a shameful period in history. Since having met Roisin, she felt closer to it all and in a way ashamed for the way the English government had behaved. Roisin was a survivor of that misery. She felt determined to find out whether she had made it back to the village and if indeed the village was still there.

Whenever Alexa went into Falmouth, she felt tempted to make contact with Philip Warren to see if he had any news. There had been nothing in the national newspapers or on TV. The discovery of a Lorna Doone encampment on Dartmoor would surely have made headlines.

Philip had put his job on the line by helping to return Roisin to her home and she would not betray him. He had promised Alexa he would contact her if there were any developments and so far she had heard nothing.

The time went by so quickly at the cottage. In between art and writing, she painted the rooms of the cottage and installed a few modern updates like a shower and new flooring in the bathroom. Although a good few years away, her intention on retirement was to live in Cornwall permanently. The wonderful countryside, one or two neighbours, a local village, more people she had yet to meet. *I really ought to find out more about Cornwall,* she thought.

Her first port of call was Jenny at the farm next door.

'Hullo there,' she cried, giving Alexa a hug. 'Haven't seen you for a while. How are you? I've been a bit busy with the calves up at Top Farm lately. What happened to your girl from the moor?'

'I don't know,' replied Alexa. 'Philip the policeman set her on her way. He knows the moor very well. We were going along the track and suddenly she pushed her way through the bushes and disappeared. We can only hope she recognised her surroundings and made her way home.'

'Want a cup of tea?'

'Please. Never say no to a cuppa.'

Jenny scurried about and came back with two mugs of tea. 'What then? Tell all.'

'Nothing. Haven't heard a word. I am glad really. I don't want them found. Where would they go?'

'Prison, I suspect. Some do-gooder reporting them for not paying Council tax or trespassing.'

'Oh God. I hope not. I had better start honing up on local law.'

'Would you really go to court for them?' asked Jenny in astonishment.

'Yes, I would. You have no idea what these people have been through.'

'Good luck then. Now I've got to go and see to those calves.'

Alexa went back to the cottage in thoughtful mood. Right. I must start integrating, getting to know the locals.

Once again making sure the cats were safe, Alexa got in the car and drove to the nearest village.

The only grocery store was a surprise. It was large, stocked with around fifty different sorts of whisky, high class foods like smoked salmon, a dozen sorts of cheese and prices to match. This was odd. She had understood that the local folk were not too well off.

'Good morning, Madam,' a large genial-looking man addressed her. 'What can I get for you?' His accent was educated with only a touch of Cornish burr.

'Ham please. Local if you've got it; more flavour than that dry supermarket stuff.'

'Locally cured. That suit you? You on holiday?' he asked as he picked up a joint of smoked ham.

'Not quite,' she replied. 'I have a cottage near Porth Abbas next to Jenny at the farm.'

He paused, slices of ham poised midway between the bacon slicer and the scales. 'You must be the cat lady. I've heard about you.'

'Oh Lord,' she replied. 'Well, we don't use the broomstick a lot. Two cats on the end would push me up in the air and make us a bit off-balance.'

She looked up hesitantly. He suddenly burst out laughing. 'A sense of humour,' he said.

'Do you work down here?'

'No. I work just outside London.'

'Why don't you move down here? You seem to like it.'

'I should love to move here but my sort of work isn't available in Cornwall and retirement a good way off.'

'What is your sort of work, if you don't mind my asking?'

Alexa hesitated only because it always seemed a bit pompous, a bit show-off. 'I am a medical research scientist.'

'Clever stuff. What are you researching?'

'Thrombosis, the inherited sort at the moment. May I ask you something?' said Alexa looking up into the shopkeeper's face. 'I had better introduce myself. I'm Alexa.' She proffered her hand.

'I'm Robert. I'd shake your hand but not with a slice of ham in it. What did you want to ask?'

'Well. I feel embarrassed now.'

'Go on.'

'My impression is that the inhabitants of this village are not very well off. Your beautiful shop doesn't quite fit the picture.'

'No. You are quite right. I am afraid the locals get the bus into Falmouth and shop at the supermarket. It's the folk from the big houses around that demand the provisions I provide. They want it. I sell it.' Rob turned to face Alexa. 'You are a perceptive young lady. You see more than beautiful scenery and craft shops.'

'In the old days,' she replied, 'it was the rich landowners controlling the tin mines, the china clay, the fishing that kept the people poor. Now it is the financial types flashing their money and buying up the properties as holiday homes while the locals act as cleaners and gardeners.'

'That sounds a rather cynical view.'

'Yes. I suppose it is even if I am one who benefits from the situation. It would be interesting to find out how the changes came about.'

'You should talk to Thomas Banham,' he said, wrapping up the ham in waxed paper. 'He's a historian, nice man. He'll tell you a lot more than I can. He's a friend of mine. I'll give him a ring if you like. He drinks in the local pub You could meet him there.'

'Thank you. I should like that. I must be going. I'll come by broomstick next time, only one cat. Should make parking a bit easier.'

She paid for the ham and went out of the shop smiling broadly.

Robert shook his head. *Don't know what to make of her*, he thought. *Is she clever or dotty?*

True to his word, Robert phoned Alexa who was walking over the top field so had a reasonable mobile signal. She sat on a convenient hummock of grass and opened up her phone.

Chapter 7

'Hullo cat lady.'

'That has to be Rob.'

'Only teasing. I spoke to Tom Banham. He would be delighted to meet you. There is a coffee morning, sale, whatever, on Saturday at the Lobster pub in the village and he suggested you meet there, and he can introduce you to some of the locals. I am sure a touch of London would be welcome. Bit of outside news, a change from the local gossip.'

'Should I take something for the sale?'

'That be nice. I am sure it would be appreciated.'

'Hm. I'll see what I can find. What does Tom Banham look like?'

'He looks like a historian. Goatee beard, tweed jacket. Can't miss him.'

'OK. I suppose you can't come?'

''Fraid not. Can't leave the shop. Have to earn a crust.'

'Thanks for calling. See you sometime. Bye.'

Walking back to the cottage, she thought, *I must sort out my questions for Tom and what on earth can I take to sell?*

Tin mines, china clay, fishing. Those were the topics she would like to learn about.

Don't be pushy Alexa. Let Tom do the talking.

Saturday morning came. She was quite excited. It would be nice to meet some of the locals, learn what activities she could join when she eventually moved here permanently.

Now. What to wear? Jeans, shirt, sweater, casual loafer shoes. After much thought, she decided on a painting for the sale. She was a good amateur artist, had sold a few, had a couple in a London gallery. She selected a view of the creek at dawn. She had had to get up very early to catch the light. *I hope they don't think I am showing off.*

After making sure the cats were safe, she drove down to the pub. There were a number of stalls outside displaying a wide range of goods. She liked the look of the vegetables. She would buy some later on. And books; she must definitely see what was going there.

'Hello, my dear,' said a lady with a soft Cornish accent standing behind a table laden with an eclectic selection of china. 'Now what can I sell you?'

'I want a bit of everything but first I have arranged to meet Tom Banham.'

'The professor we call him. You'll find him inside. There's tea and coffee there and you should try a scone with jam and cream.'

'Sounds delicious. Now jam first then cream in Cornwall. Is that the right way round? I brought something for the sale. Who do I give that to?'

'What is it? Can I have a look?'

Alexa nervously handed over her painting. 'I'm Alexa,' she said.

'You must be the cat lady.'

'Oh dear. My reputation has preceded me.'

'No, no. I think it's lovely. I like cats. Oh my, that is beautiful.' She pulled the painting out of the bag. 'Did you do it?'

'Yes, it's just a hobby.'

'Evelyn, come and look at this.'

Evelyn came over. 'That's lovely. Davey, he's the publican, will be so pleased with that.'

Alexa went into the pub. There was a stuffed fish in a glass case, a miner's lamp, a lobster pot by the fireplace and paintings of Cornish sailing ships on the walls. A good, old-fashioned inn. She could imagine it in the winter with a roaring log fire.

Walking over to the man behind the bar, 'You must be Davey. The ladies said to see you with this,' as she handed over her sale offering.

He was tall with a ruddy complexion and a short, grey beard, *An ex-fisherman*, she thought.

'This for the sale? Did you do it?'

'Yes.' With a slightly embarrassed air. 'I hope it's OK.'

'It's bootiful. You're good. I'd like that on the wall here in the pub. But I'd probably get a better price for it one the galleries in Folkestone or Porthleven, if you don't mind.'

'I am not a resident of Cornwall so I am not allowed to sell here.'

'A mate of mine will get around that one.' He laughed. 'Be a bit more for the charity.'

'Which I assume is the lifeboats,' said Alexa. 'Good cause.'

'Yes. The Penzance crew do a lot of good work. They are nearest to us.'

'Now I must get my tea and scone. I was commanded, almost, to get one.' She walked over to the cake stall and was rewarded with a scone and more clotted cream than she would normally eat in a year.

'I am looking for Tom Banham,' as she handed over a fiver. 'No. No change, thank you.'

'Tom, the professor. There he be, sitting in the corner.'

She turned and saw a distinguished looking man nursing a pint of beer. He was just as Rob had said: tweed jacket, goatee beard.

She made her way over indelicately balancing the massive scone and cup of tea. 'Hello. I'm Alexa. Rob said I would find you here.'

'Tom.' He held out his hand for her to shake. 'Shall I relieve you of the scone before it hits the floor?'

'You can eat half of it if you like.'

'Doesn't mix too well with beer. Sit down. Have a seat.' He pulled a chair out from the table.

'I gather you are interested in the demise of Cornwall,' he said.

'Yes. I am curious to know why in a not too wealthy village there is a shop that's a bit like Fortnum and Mason. That sounds frightfully snobbish. Sorry.'

'Don't be. It is all a part of the rundown of Cornish Industry; fishing, tin mining, china clay. You obviously have an enquiring mind. What's your job?'

'I'm a medical research scientist. Please keep it to yourself. You only have to mention the word medical, and people start asking you about their warts or their piles. I do some clinical work. I like that part of it best.'

Tom gave a bellowing laugh. People turned to look. 'Not a word,' he said, 'but it does explain your interest.'

'As soon as the catch was landed, the fish were baulked, as it was termed. That is, put into barrels of salt to preserve them. Part of the catch was pressed down by hand to release the oil mainly used for lighting lamps. One barrel of around three thousand pilchards would produce eight to nine gallons of oil. In eighteen ninety, the huge seine nets were changed to small nets cast off from much smaller ships with a limit of six men to a boat. In 1850, over-fishing had led to a huge decrease in the catch. Nearer to our time pilchards became unpopular. Tastes change. Remember those tins of pilchards in tomato sauce?'

Alexa screwed up her face. 'I'd rather not. Weren't they awful? We used to be given them in sandwiches. I can still smell them.'

'Then some bright spark in the restaurant business,' continued Tom. 'Renamed them Cornish sardines, sprinkled them with lemon juice or whatever and they were flavour of the month. The catch went up to seventy tonnes in the mid-nineties and Cornwall is reaping the benefit.'

Alexa looked up from her notepad where she had been scribbling at high speed. 'Thanks Tom. I understand a lot more now.'

'You are welcome. Let's leave the herrings till next time. It will be a chance to chat again. Another drink?'

'I'll get them,' she said. 'Beer again? And a coffee for me.' Alexa walked across to the bar.

'You seem to be getting on well with the professor then,' said the coffee lady.

'Yes. He's a nice man. I'm Alexa.'

'I'm Dorothy.'

'What was all that chat about?' she half looked at Alexa hoping for a bit of gossip.

'Pilchards.'

'What?' as she nearly dropped the cup of coffee.

'Yes. Pilchards. It's herrings next time. Should be interesting. You should listen in.'

Alexa could hardly carry the beer and the coffee back to the table; she was shaking with laughter.

'Well, what's the joke?' asked Tom as he took the glass and sampled a mouthful of beer.

'Dorothy thinks we are carrying on and asked what we were chatting about. You should have seen her face when I said pilchards.'

Tom guffawed and everyone turned to look. 'Oh dear. I wonder what they will make of herrings?'

Alexa suddenly felt a great affection for these people who, clearly not rich, that they would give their time and whatever they could spare for the lifeboat fund. She also felt slightly embarrassed. The ladies were neatly but poorly dressed, and she was sitting there in her weekend gear of designer jeans and cashmere sweater. They worked as hard as she did, but their rewards were so much less in monetary terms but maybe greater in others.

She finished her coffee, thanked Tom again for his help and went around the stalls going off with a large collection of fresh vegetables and several books.

'Goodbye everybody. See you again,' she called out and certainly intended to.

Back at her flat in the Home Counties, Alexa went to work, worried about Ivan who was getting old and had been poorly recently and wondered how many more times she would take him to Cornwall. She continued to spend time on furthering her knowledge on the fishing problems of the Falmouth area, sometimes thinking what an odd subject to be investigating, but once started she had wanted to know more.

She didn't get back to Cornwall for some months, making a visit to Rob at the shop a priority.

'Good morning, cat lady. How are you?'

'Miaow,' she replied. 'Does Tom still visit the pub? I am due my next lecture.'

'Yes. I'll give him a ring and see when he is going next. Did you come by broomstick?'

'No; it looked like rain, and the cats are arguing whose turn it is.' She laughed. 'Bye. Thank you.'

A week later found her sitting at a table with Tom. 'Want some gin in that tonic?'

'No thanks. I am one of those tiresome people who can't drink alcohol.'

'Now about the herrings,' pronounced Tom as though he was about to start a lecture to a learned society. 'They were fished as far back as the time of King John and Elizabeth the first. I am not sure when the tradition started but a lookout would be watching and when he saw the shoal approaching he would cry Hevva, Hevva, to let the fisherman know the fish were on their way. The huge nets with corks attached would be dragged into the sea, then tightened when the nets were loaded and dragged ashore. It must have been hard, cold and heavy work.'

I bet all those little bones stuck in Elizabeth 1st's rather rotten teeth, she thought. *Though I suppose a servant would be employed to pick them out for her.*

'In more recent times, herrings were mostly caught in Scotland but Cornwall also fished for them. Like most species, they had suffered from overfishing. In the eighteen hundreds, the system of bussing was allowed. These bigger boats with large square sails extended the fishing range so consequently the herring numbers suffered. This was abandoned after a while and there was a return to luggers with their smaller sails and greater speed. Steamboats contributed to the problems. There were many causes for the decline of the herring. An "Exclusive Fishing Zone" was set up in nineteen 1977 which helped the situation.'

'The British were never very keen on herrings preferring to eat them smoked as kippers. Their main catch these days is sold to the Dutch who consume them in vast quantities.'

'In 1980, herrings were declared over fished and the battle for the rights continues. Our matchmaker isn't here today. She might like to get an interest in mackerel,' said Tom.

'She might like to get news of our imagined affair,' replied Alexa.

'Mackerel have also been fished for hundreds of years,' Tom continued. 'They were mostly caught with drift nets from luggers but never on a Sunday. The people of Newlyn were very religious, mostly serious Methodists, who believed it was wrong to land catch on the Sabbath. Other fleets quickly exploited the situation getting into the vacant harbour space causing great anger resulting in serious riots along the coast at Porthleven, Mousehole, St Ives as well as Newlyn. An interesting point about the mackerel which mostly come from the Atlantic is that they gather together in huge shoals as they come to warmer waters and force the smaller fish up into a broiling mass on the surface.'

'I bet that was a sight to see,' Alexa interrupted.

'One Sunday,' Tom continued, 'tempers spilled over when a number of catches were landed in Newlyn by crews from other ports taking advantage of the situation. The local fishermen retaliated, throwing all the fish from non-Cornish vessels into the harbour. The police and the army were called in to control the situation. The east coast fishermen continued to work on a Sunday. Eventually, the situation was brought under control and Newlyn today is a flourishing port handling large catches every day of the week. Had enough of fish?' queried Tom.

'No, no. I'm fascinated. It is kind of you to pass on all your knowledge. I have learned so much. I'll get us more drinks.'

They touched glasses and drank.

'I am attempting to write a book. Don't suppose it will ever be published but it keeps me off the streets.' She looked at him and smiled.

'I shall expect a signed copy then.'

'I shall acknowledge your help.'

'The other major industry which led to Cornwall's wealth was the discovery of china clay, not my subject, I'm afraid,' said Tom.

'You will know more than I do so anything will be helpful.'

'The huge heaps, almost mountains are evidence of the clay industry at St Austell. William Cookworthy first discovered clay or kaolin in Cornwall in 1746. There were a few deposits around the world. The Chinese had been using it for a thousand years to make pure white porcelain but their clay in no way compared with the amount or quality of the Cornish find.'

'In 1768, Cookworthy patented a new method and opened his own porcelain factory. Kaolin was also used for whitening paper and is still the primary use for it today. Early in the twentieth century, there was a downturn. Wages were low and conditions poor for the workers. In 1919, three producers combined to buy fifty per cent of the rights to mine and this partnership is the main provider today, most of the clay being used in paper manufacture.'

'Well,' gasped Alexa, 'it seems to me you know an awful lot about it. Thank you so much. All I have to do now is write the book. I shan't be down for a while, but I hope we can meet up again. Bye,' she said and made for the door.

'Bye,' Tom replied, 'it has been an interesting interlude.'

With work and worrying about Ivan, Alexa put aside the book project but one evening the thought came into her mind. *How was Roisin? Did she find her way back to her family?* She wouldn't be writing a book just yet, too much to do but the knowledge was stored away for when she had the time. Hopefully, Roisin had slipped back into secluded village life, sowing, reaping the harvest, milking the cows and goats; a life unchanged for centuries.

I would not have started getting interested in the industries of Cornwall thought had it not been for Roisin's fascination with Falmouth harbour and the great ships that went out all over the world. But it has been interesting, I must admit and satisfied my curiosity for a while.

Chapter 8

One evening, at home in the flat near London, Alexa made a bold decision. 'I shall go to Northern Ireland for a few days,' she announced to the cats. Seeing the sites where the John James Kelly family had lived and suffered would perhaps bring more understanding of why the last James Kelly had finally given up and made the decision to try for a better life in England. If nothing else, she could visit a couple of the graveyards and pay her respects.

Why, she wondered, did she always take the troubles of the world (or a small piece of it) on to her shoulders? Why did she feel responsible for other people's problems and feel obliged to help? It was a vicious circle. Once you had sorted an issue, the next one came along. The local people came to her. 'You helped my friend. Could you help me?' and so more letters to write, another visit to the Citizens Advice Centre.

She was not a saint, a bit of a mug really. She sometimes tried to analyse herself. The nearest conclusion was that her mother always helped the world and his wife, so she had followed in her footsteps or was, she paused in contemplation, trying to win the approval of her father.

Her mother had an instinctive goodness. Alexa had fond memories of her.

'I shall book. I shall stay in Belfast and go to the Titanic Museum, take a trip to the Giant's Causeway and then go out to Ballycona to see the remains of the old farmhouse and visit the graveyard. I might even hire a car and drive down to Skibbereen in Cork to walk over the fields where so many thousands are buried or, she paused, I might do it the other way round, Skibbereen first so that I end up with pleasant memories of this now green and much more pleasant land.'

At the earliest opportunity, Alexa took herself to a local holiday booking office. Several assistants were seated at a long desk gazing avidly at their computers. She went over to a stand of brochures and starting sorting leaflets for Ireland. She half turned and out of the corner of her eye selected the assistant with the most friendly face. She settled for one, a pretty girl with long fair hair.

Going over to the counter, she gave a slight cough and said, 'I should like to book a short trip to Belfast around June or July, please.'

The girl looked up and smiled. 'Yes Madam. There is a very good three-day package that includes flight, hotel and a couple of trips, one to the Giant's Causeway and the other to the Titanic Museum, which I am told is fantastic.'

'Oh dear.' Alexa's thoughts dwelt briefly on the Titanic. 'I am not too sure I want to experience more sadness but if it is included in the package, I suppose I may as well go. That's sounds like a good deal. Can you book it for me?'

'Yes, of course,' replied the young lady as she looked up and smiled, then started whizzing around the computer keyboard.

'Name, address, phone number, email. Do you have a valid passport?'

'Yes, but I didn't think it was needed. Northern Ireland is part of the UK.'

'It is better to have one. They sometimes ask for it as you book in, and you may want to go into Eire.'

'Well. Yes, my passport is up to date. I travel abroad quite a bit,' replied Alexa.

On and on it went. *She will want the cats' birthdays next*, she thought. *It had seemed easier to get to the Gambia, though I did have a backup team of secretaries to help.*

'Can I hire a car for a couple of days?' she queried, thinking, *I can get out to Ballycona and drive down to Skibbereen.*

'There's a garage near the hotel. You can arrange it there, or tell me what day and what type of car and I can arrange it for you.'

'Small car, automatic, please.'

'Now I have to ask you to pay. Debit or credit?' The girl smiled as though softening the blow.

Alexa inserted her debit card and paid up. *Oh well. It's done now, education rather than enjoyment. I think I'll try to make it a bit of a holiday.*

I need a cup of coffee, she thought as she walked out of the shop. There should be enough money left in the bank for that, and to prove the point, went into the nearest café and ordered a sandwich and an Americano, milk on the side.

She needed to do this, visit the sites of the Potato Famine, the museums, the graveyards and try to track down the old farmhouse where Roisin's ancestors had lived and so many had died. This girl appearing out of the mist had affected Alexa more than she sometimes realised, got under her skin, so she now felt it was almost her duty to find out why, so long after what is now known as the

Great Hunger, she felt it her mission to find out why the current James Kelly had left Ireland.

But for now, she must concentrate on Ivan. He had grown very thin and was no longer the annoying, playful cat he normally was. After a visit to the vet, Alexa came to the sad conclusion that it was time to let him go. She booked a couple of days leave; she knew she would howl like a baby at his passing and wished to be left alone to recover.

She kissed him goodbye and put him into the basket. At the surgery, she handed the basket over to the vet who said, 'He won't feel any pain.'

After about five minutes, the vet came and put the limp little body in her arms. She held him close then put him in his basket and took him home to bury him in the garden. Surrounding the grave with some stones she had brought back from Cornwall and laying a bunch of flowers from the garden the ceremony was complete.

Arrogant, funny, beautiful Ivan with his big blue eyes was gone. He had lived a good life with Fluff as a companion, gone on holiday to Cornwall twice a year. What more could a cat have asked for?

Fluff was bewildered, wandering around looking for Ivan. She attached herself more closely to Alexa, following at her heels as she walked around the garden, sitting on her lap the moment she sat down. Even animals grieve she thought as she buried her face in Fluff's black, silky fur and shed more tears.

Alexa remembered hearing an interview on radio with Michael Bentine who had tragically suffered the loss of three of his children, two daughters and a son. When asked how he coped, he said he shut himself away and cried until there were no more tears to shed. Only then could he face the world.

How can I compare my situation with that? Alexa asked herself. There was no comparison. But Ivan was part of her family and she mourned him. She dried her eyes and got on with her life. Due back at work in a couple of days, she wanted to present her usual efficient if not always calm self with no air of tragedy. She would tell no one.

Chapter 9

In June, after handing over Fluff into the tender care of Mrs Nicholls, Alexa took a taxi to Luton Airport for an early flight to Belfast. She joined the long queue to the booking desk and eventually got her boarding pass. Her case on wheels was small enough to go onto the baggage rack on the plane which would speed things up at the other end. The majority of the passengers seemed to be businessmen thoroughly used to the procedure, so she attached herself to a small group and lined up behind them to have her case searched. Almost everything was turned out in the hunt for bombs and guns. So much for neat packing she thought but it was necessary; there were still troubles in Ireland.

Finally through to the other side into the departure area, she got herself a cup of coffee and waited for the tannoy call for her flight. Just over an hour and a half later, Alexa arrived at Belfast City airport. A short taxi ride took her to a friendly hotel. No soldiers with guns patrolling the streets, no lurid paintings on the buildings. She recalled the Belfast of some years ago. She had been asked to lecture at the university and arrived totally unaware of the conditions at the time. Nightly she saw on the television news crowds of youths throwing stones at the police, people being shot. It was one thing to see at a distance; a different kettle of fish to be caught up in it.

A young man holding up a placard with her name on it ushered her to a taxi and they had both got in. A few hundred yards down the road soldiers had appeared at the car window and told her to get out of the car. She was searched, the boot and inside of the car were inspected in detail. Alexa was left standing on the pavement with a gun pointed at her. She thought she was being kidnapped, at least. She felt sick and frightened. At last, they were allowed to move on. A quarter of a mile further on the same thing happened, then twice more until they reached the university entrance.

Her companion looked totally unfazed.

'What on earth is going on?' asked Alexa.

'Stormont is being reopened today,' he replied. 'This is life in Belfast. You get used to it.'

'I doubt it,' she replied.

She gave her lecture to a group of students, had another cup of coffee and a sandwich courtesy of the University, and prepared to return to the airport.

'Thank you for coming. You picked the wrong day,' offered an older, weary-looking man as she prepared to shake his hand in farewell.

'Not my choice of the day but I hope they learned something,' replied Alexa.

They were stopped only twice on the way back to the airport which she supposed was an improvement.

On the plane, she thought about the day. She was totally confused. Certainly, she been to the university but of the route there and back she could not recall a thing. She could no way find the road there and back to the airport than fly of her own volition. But that was a few years ago; the situation seemed less aggressive now.

Back to the present day; she was greeted with, 'Good morning madam' by the young man at the hotel reception desk.

'We'll just book you in then I'll show you to your room.' His speech had that delightful upturn at the end of a sentence so typical of Northern Ireland. 'Will you be doing any sightseeing while you are here? I can recommend the Titanic Museum; it's fantastic.'

'So I hear. I have a ticket booked as part of the package, thank you. I am also going to the Giant's Causeway; and I have booked a hire car for a day. I hope to get down to Ballycona and visit the graves of my ancestors.'

'Right. The garage is just across the street from the hotel. Will I show you up your room now? Here, give me your case.'

The room, overlooking the street, was comfortably furnished with a television and en suite bathroom.

That'll do me for a couple of nights, she thought. She unpacked her few belongings, changed into more casual gear and prepared to go out and once more get a coffee and a sandwich. She seemed to be living on takeaway food.

Back at the desk, she asked, 'Can I book a taxi for the Titanic Museum in half an hour's time?' she said to the young man at the desk. 'I'll wait for it outside the hotel.'

'Of course, madam. Enjoy the museum.'

'Is this your first visit to Belfast?' the taxi driver asked, half turning his head.

74

'No,' she replied. 'I was here a few years ago; it seems a much nicer place now. It was a bit frightening then.'

'Things are more peaceful now since the Good Friday agreement but we still have a way to go. Well, there you are,' as the taxi came to a halt and Alexa stared out at the most extraordinary building she had ever seen. She paid the fare plus a good tip and got out of the taxi.

'Isn't it grand?' said the driver winding down the window. 'Enjoy your visit. Call me again,' as he handed her a card with name and phone number.

Alexa stood looking at this odd-shaped, shining silver edifice opposite. She had thought the Gaudi buildings in Barcelona bizarre, but this was something else. It seems the wrong shape for a ship she thought with its two-pointed structures either side of a central block. The whole thing was silver coloured, overlaid with even brighter waves, if that is what they were. It was certainly striking, amazing, like nothing else she had ever seen, not easily forgotten.

She crossed the road, noticing the long queue of people snaking around the area waiting to get in, thankful she had booked her ticket back in England. She went through the central door, handed in her ticket and was let through into an area with large photos, souvenirs for sale and a notice inviting her to take the tour.

She took a lift to the top then started on the downward route. The first part was all about boat building. She went on; more artefacts and photos appeared. Alexa began to feel panicky, somewhat claustrophobic, as the staircase led down and down so she turned and hurriedly went back the way she had come. She was not good at enclosed places and just wanted out. Back on the ground floor she paused for a few minutes to recover then got up and pushed past a group of surprised people, past the exit sign to the tour, and going the wrong way, to find more pictures of passengers struggling into small boats and the famous one of the Titanic's last moments as she slid at an acute angle into the depths of the ocean.

'Where do you think you're going?' shouted an outraged man. 'Pay for your ticket the same as we've had to.' Alexa took one last look at the sinking Titanic, turned and fled. She had had enough of enclosure and tragedy and made for the main exit and fresh air. She crossed the road and stared once again at the extraordinary building opposite.

Consulting the guidebook, she found that there was one massive hull surrounded by four smaller ones, each the height of Titanic, one at each corner.

Titanic Museum, Belfast

The metal panels originally used in building the great liner, were represented by thousands of shards on the outside of the building which sparkled and shimmered particularly when caught by the sun. 'And I thought they were waves,' she muttered. *They look more like tears to me, the crying of the world for all the people who were lost in this terrible tragedy,* she thought. *Come on, Alexa, you are being melodramatic.* The statue with outstretched arms on the front of the building complemented the whole; it must look magnificent lit up at night. *Sometimes colours are directed at it, I am told. I should like to see that. I'll save it for my next visit. But I shall not go back inside*, feeling a bit queasy at the thought of it. Looking at the last White Star liner moored opposite, *Interesting,* she thought. 'But not interesting enough to pay it a visit. I'll walk back,' she muttered to herself. It was a straight road and hadn't seemed very far in the taxi and she could do with the fresh air.'

She set off, looking at the shops and cafes, and arrived back at the hotel in time for afternoon tea. *I shall rest until dinner, go to bed early, watch some TV, sleep, hopefully, then set off on the journey down to Skibbereen tomorrow.*

Earlier, when she had called into the garage to check whether the car would be ready for her, the mechanic was sitting at a desk going through paperwork. Hearing the door open and close, he turned around in his chair and called, 'Can I help you?'

Alexa found herself facing a good-looking man, early middle-age, she guessed. 'I have ordered a car for tomorrow and just wanted to check you have got it in hand,' she said.

He ran his finger down the list. 'What name is it?'

'Moray.'

'Yes, all in order.'

'What time do you open?' she asked. 'I should like to make an early start.'

'Well. I get here about seven; early enough? Where are you going if you don't mind my asking?'

'Skibbereen,' she volunteered.

'Skibbereen?' He stared at Alexa as though she had grown horns. 'What do you want to go there for? It's all flat land and graveyards. No one goes there for pleasure. Are you a historian or writer or something?' His query ended on the attractive uplift of speech. His face suddenly coloured up. 'I'm sorry; it's nothing to do with me.'

'That's alright. Let's just say I am an interested party. Something I have to do.'

'It's a very long drive, seems to go on forever. I had to deliver a car there a few years ago. It seemed even longer coming back by coach. My name is Lorcan, by the way. If it is any help, I'll give you the keys now and leave the car outside the garage then you can start when you want.'

'That would be very helpful. I'm Alexa. What is the best route? I've got a map but the locals usually know best.'

He thought for a bit then said, 'Go to the end of this road,' pointing right. 'And follow the signs for Dublin. It's a bit of a devil getting through the city. The sooner they get on and build this motorway they are always talking about the better. You could take the smaller roads, but it adds quite a good few miles to your journey. Follow the signs for Cork then look out for the coastal road to Skibbereen. I seem to remember going through a place called Clonkilt, something like that. No. Clonakilty, that's it; not exactly a swinging town. Then drive and drive and eventually, you'll get there.'

Lorcan looked straight at Alexa. 'Good luck,' he said, 'I'm curious to know why you want to visit such a godforsaken place.'

'I might tell you one day,' she smiled. 'At the present time, it might bring harm to a group of people.' She smiled at him. 'Thanks for your help, Lorcan. What a lovely name.'

'I'll look after your car,' he said.

She turned and left the shop.

Alexa returned to the hotel and arranged to have a packet of sandwiches and a flask of coffee ready for early next morning.

The young man looked surprised at the request. 'My...' he replied. 'You're an early riser, so you are. Yes. I'll have that ready for you.'

She ate an early dinner then went back to her room to pack her camera, notebook and pens. Getting into bed, she set the alarm for half past four and fell asleep, exhausted with the day's happenings.

It was still dark when she crept downstairs, dressed warmly and wearing stout boots to collect her supplies for the day.

'Good luck to wherever you're going,' said the night porter. 'You drive carefully now.'

'I will. Thank you,' she replied.

Alexa opened up the car outside the garage; it was cold inside and the windscreen covered with dew. She turned on the heater and waited for the car to warm up and the windscreen to clear. After driving up the road to get the feel of the car, she turned and set off for her long journey south.

There was little traffic on the road at that time of the morning. Dublin was a confusing mass of roads and road signs. As the sky grew lighter there were more and more cars and bicycles as people made their way to work. Eventually a sign for Cork appeared. With relief, she followed this as it turned into a country road bordered by the endless green fields. She stopped, opened the window and drank some coffee now growing a bit cool.

Lorcan was right; *It is a long, long way*, she thought, *but having got this far I am determined to get to the end.*

She followed a sign for Clonakilty, a small straggling village. The tang of sea air drifted in through the windows and looking left she could see in the far distance a patch of grey blue which was the Atlantic curving in to the coastline. On and on, the monotony broken only by an isolated farmhouse, straggling groups of cottages, with sometimes a village store.

A weathered signpost pointing down a narrow road to Skibbereen at last appeared. She followed it through more endless fields and found herself approaching a roundabout.

Following a pointer to Abbeystrewry she slowly drove on awhile then stopped the car. When she got out she was so stiff, she could barely walk. She looked around; a cluster of gravestones surrounding what remained of a ruined church, on a piece of rising land hardly visible through the mist. A low brick wall surrounded all, green fields fading into the distance. My God. What a forlorn and desperate place.

So this was the area where the local populace had staggered into at night at the time of the Great Hunger to bring the latest bodies of those who had died during the day, some on farm carts, some carried on the shoulders of their family who had barely enough strength to walk themselves. There was scarcely enough soil to cover the dead; so many had lain with not much more than a sprinkling of earth over them for many years. It is said that at least ten thousand lie here, victims of hunger and the diseases which in their weakened state they were unable to resist.

Alexa walked over to examine some of the gravestones, then suddenly sickened and saddened, she walked back to the car, got in and drove away into the village of Skibbereen.

As Lorcan had said, it was hardly a swinging town; indeed it was hardly a town. In the village shop, the kindly man behind the counter refilled her flask in the kitchen behind the shop. 'Coffee to go' was only just emerging in the city.

'Do many visitors come here?' enquired Alexa.

'Not many. Historians mostly,' he replied. 'To look at the graveyards. Sometimes I think I am earning a living on the backs of the dead. My ancestors survived here; I am not sure how. Things may pick up one day.' Shrugging his shoulders, he suddenly smiled. 'Do you know the story of Tom Guerin?'

'No,' Alexa replied. 'Who is he? Tell me about him.'

'Three-year-old Tom was thought to be dead and was thrown on to the cart with a pile of bodies to be delivered to Abbeystrewry At the graveyard he was pushed onto the ground, covered with a minimum of soil and received a hit by a shovel in the process. Tom groaned and was hauled out from under the earth badly injured but alive. Crippled, he survived until he was sixty-five, most of his life trading on "the boy brought back from the dead".'

'Fascinating,' said Alexa. 'Well, at least one slightly happy story. I must be on my way.'

Driving back to the graveyard close to the ruined church, she began to look for the name Kelly on the gravestones and rubbing at the moss, she finally found a K, the writing hardly visible. At last, she had found the graves of the last two of the Kelly family to be buried in what is now consecrated ground. Most of the family remains were buried or thrown down near the village of Ballycona but, she understood a few had trekked south in the hope of better conditions only to find that sickness and hunger had preceded them. She stood looking for a while then moved over to the area with a notice board declaring, 'Here lie victims of the Great Hunger.' *So, this is where the bodies were thrown nightly, too many to have a decent burial*, she thought, the relatives too weak and too poor to give them one. Years later, the bodies were covered with soil and Christian prayers said over them.

Driving to a quiet spot just beyond the village, she settled down under a blanket for a couple of hours sleep. She felt quite safe. There wasn't a living soul in sight. As she dozed off, she thought that she had fulfilled the promise to herself; to visit this godawful place, for the Kellys, for Roisin, for the thousands who died, who had deserved a better fate than starvation.

She woke up thick-headed, opened the window to let in some air and started on the long road back.

Ignoring the sign to Clonakilty and the long route via the coast she pressed on to Cork, then Dublin, then at last Belfast turning off at the sign for Ballycona. Beyond a scattering of small farms she found the church. Two Kellys had headstones in what was the main churchyard. Of the children's graves there was no sign and she had to assume they had been buried with the rest in the unconsecrated ground beyond.

Back in the car finally, to her relief, she saw a sign for Belfast. She made her way up the road to the hotel, stopped outside the garage and parked the car.

Though it was late, Lorcan was still working.

'How was the journey?' he asked.

'Long, tedious, as you predicted.'

'Did you find what you wanted?'

'Yes, thank you. Once is enough. I'll not do that again.'

'You are welcome. Go get yourself some dinner and a good night's rest.' He hesitated. 'Come back some day and tell me why you went; it is such a curious place to visit.'

She handed over the keys. 'I will come back. Thanks for your help, Lorcan.' She smiled and left.

Tottering into the hotel. 'Just in time for dinner,' said the cheerful young waiter. 'I recommend the lamb chops.'

'Lovely. I'll have a quick wash and brush up and be down.'

Dinner revived her somewhat and retiring to her room, she thought, *Did it*. And now for some sleep as she fell exhausted into bed. Lying awake for a short while she asked herself whether this obsession with the Kellys was a tad too far. She would let the matter rest for a while.

She woke to traffic noise and weak sunshine trying to break through a grey sky. Feeling stiff and sore she stood under the shower and let the water run over for a few minutes. Having got dressed, she packed her case ready for the homeward journey early evening, humped her luggage into the lift, and handed it over to the desk clerk for safe storage.

'Are you away home today?' he enquired.

'Well, first I have a visit to the Giant's Causeway,' she replied.

'You'll enjoy that, amazing place geologically. The guides will tell you all the legends which, in my view, are more entertaining. Get yourself a good breakfast and away with you and have a good day.'

Feeling fortified with porridge, toast, marmalade and coffee, she put on her coat and walked down to the coach station. There was an excited crowd waiting to board and Alexa chatted to some of them. They were mostly, like her, on a short tourist trip and seemed surprised to have found Northern Ireland so attractive.

An elderly lady came up to Alexa and started chatting.

'Did you know we'll be calling in at the Bushmills Distillery on the way?' she said.

'Oh good. We can all get drunk before dinner then. Come on. Let's sit together. By the accent, you come from Norther Ireland?'

'Yes. From the west coast so this part of the country is all new to me. I am looking forward to seeing the Giant's Causeway.'

'I believe the west is very beautiful, very dramatic scenery?' queried Alexa.

'It is; great cliffs and huge waves crashing in. I love it but it is not for everybody. Life can be quite hard.'

They all piled into the coach, the old lady sitting next to Alexa, and set off for the distillery.

'I am Alexa.'

'And I am Erin,' replied her companion.

The coach turned through large gates and parked.

'We are only staying twenty minutes,' called out the driver. 'Just time to buy your goods and not get drunk.'

The distillery part was interesting but as a non-drinker, Alexa was more interested in the gift shop. She purchased a bottle of malt for Mrs Nicholls and a box of whisky fudge for herself and it was time to get back to the coach. Erin seemed loaded with goodies by the clinking sound in her bag.

Yes, thought Alexa. *Quite a few nights by a turf fire. Good luck to her.*

'We are now approaching the Giant's Causeway,' announced the driver. 'I'll see you back here in two hours. Enjoy yourselves. Listen to the legends.'

Out of the coach, all they could see was a rough road leading downhill.

'Well. Where is it then? I can't be walking a long way,' said Erin.

The answer was provided as a rather ancient-looking vehicle came trundling up the hill.

'This is the shuttle bus for the Giant's Causeway,' a voice announced. 'Let the passengers off first please.'

They all piled in and bumped and jerked their way downhill.

Before getting out once more came the voice of the driver. 'Will you just look at this?' 'Have you ever seen anything so grand?'

Once out in the fresh air, the passengers had to agree. They were surrounded by mounds of hexagonal columns of rock stretching in front and behind but mostly stretching far out into the sea beyond. It truly was an astonishing sight.

'Have a look around and then we'll gather here, and I'll tell you the history and the legends of the Causeway. Away you go and enjoy the magic.'

Alexa hung on to Erin's arm and together they climbed to the top of one of the lower mounds. 'And I haven't even opened the whisky yet,' said Erin as they staggered along.

Every piece of rock appeared to have been carved or shaped to a mathematical degree.

They wandered around and, seeing a crowd gathering, the pair carefully made their way down and joined their fellow tourists.

'Are we all here? Then I'll begin.' It was the coach driver turned guide. He was wearing an elf's hat in emerald green. Sitting on a rock slightly above his audience he started his talk. 'My name is Finn though we are not directly related. 'Geologically,' he said. 'Around fifty million years ago, there was a massive volcanic eruption which resulted in earth movement right out into the sea as far as Fingal's cave. You must all have heard of Mendelssohn's overture, that so magical, descriptive piece of music, in my and millions of others' opinion.

'Here, on this piece of land where you are standing, is the outer edge of the eruption. He waved his arm around, then pointed to the mound on which he was sitting. Beyond is the "bridge" which stretches from Northern Ireland to Scotland. But ladies and gentlemen there is more to come. Many legends grew up surrounding the Causeway and now I'll be telling you the best.'

'Typically, Irish. He can spin a yarn,' Alexa observed to Erin.

'I've heard a lot of Irish blarney before,' replied Erin; 'it should be entertaining.'

'Now Finn McCool was a warrior in Irish mythology associated with a tribe which existed long before the Celts,' he began. 'Some say he was a giant fifty-four feet tall. He was brought up in the forest in Ireland by two stepmothers. Imagine that. How would you get to the top of him to see if he had had a good wash? And two stepmothers. Surely one is enough.'

'One is quite enough for me,' called out a wag in the audience.

'Anyway, Finn challenged Benandoner (known as the Red Man), who lived in Scotland at the other end of the bridge, to a duel. Now some say that Benandoner built the bridge so he could get across to Ireland to fight Finn. Another version is that Finn didn't like getting his feet wet so he built the bridge to be above the level of the sea. What a wimp; all fifty-four feet of him. Could he not have put his wellingtons on?'

Everybody laughed.

'Another version has it that Benandoner threatened Ireland. Finn, in a rage, hurled rocks from the Antrim coast into the sea and created a pathway from Ireland to Scotland. Benandoner ran home creating a space between the two countries.'

'Will we all be getting the shuttle back now?' called out Finn minor in the silly green hat. 'Thank you ladies and gentlemen,' which drew applause from the crowd and a good many tips. A bumpy ride in the shuttle bus to the car park and transfer to the more comfortable version and they were on their way back to Belfast.

After more tips and goodbyes, Alexa gave Erin a hug. 'You have made my day more enjoyable,' she said. 'Good journey home.' *What a nice lady*, she thought.

Back at the hotel she rescued her luggage, got the receptionist to book a taxi to the airport and then said her goodbyes.

'I hope you have enjoyed your trip to Belfast,' said the young man behind the desk. 'And you'll visit us again.'

'I have enjoyed it,' replied Alexa, surprising herself. It had ended on a good note.

Then it was off to the airport and the boring formalities before boarding for the short flight back to Luton.

It was late evening when she arrived home. She paid the taxi fare adding yet another tip and was pleased to see the lights on at home. That would mean Mrs Nicholls would be there with Fluff. She rang the bell, the door opened and she was home.

'Hello dear. Did you have a good trip? I'll get you a cup of tea and you can tell me all.'

Fluff came running over to her and rubbed against her leg. Alexa picked her up and cuddled her. 'Did you miss me?' almost expecting an answer. Home two minutes and she was talking to the cats, cat, she corrected herself.

Mrs Nicholls bustled in with the tea. 'Here you are, dear. I am sure you need this.'

'It is very welcome, I assure you. Now give me all the news.'

'Mrs Clark died but she was very old.'

'Oh dear,' replied Alexa. 'How sad,' desperately trying to remember who Mrs Clark was.

'Here you are. This is from Fluff, for looking after her,' as Alexa produced the bottle of Bush Mills.

Mrs Nicholls' eyes lit up. 'Thank you, dear; it is always a pleasure to look after her.'

This was true, thought Alexa; it made a little holiday for the kind old lady. She could pop in next door, turn the heating on full, select her favour programme on the television, get Fluff ensconced on her lap and she was settled for the evening, and I don't have to worry about Fluff.

'Did you have a nice time?' queried Mrs Nicholls.

'Yes, thank you,' as she recounted the story of Finn McCool. Of the earlier part of the trip she made no mention; she would think about that part on her own.

Mrs Nicholls went home and Alexa went to bed with Fluff a few paw steps behind.

Chapter 10

With still three days left before returning to work, Alexa had been taking it easy. A few jobs around the house interspersed with numerous cups of tea it was relaxing just to potter around; a change from the rush and tear of hospital emergencies.

So on her last afternoon with a cup of tea, a packet of crisps on the side table and, of course, a cat on her lap, she started a discussion with Fluff, inevitably about her recent visit to Ireland.

'Why do I always get involved in sorting other people's problems? What do you think, Fluff?' as she affectionately stroked the cat's head who promptly turned to look up at Alexa indicating that she could do with a scratch under her chin as well.

What is the word for examination of oneself? Think hard, Alexa. Let us try Roget's Thesaurus. Got to start somewhere. I like Roget; it leads you on a journey from word to word until you hone in on one that seems appropriate and gives you pause to think.

Retrospection: is that the one I want? To look back, reflect on past events in one's own life.

She paused, considering the problem. *Well, certainly, past events have governed my life. My father's indifference to me, my trying to please him, to be noticed by him. Was this my fault? Was I one child too many? I was considered clever by non-family.*

She had lost herself in books and painting, acquiring more and more knowledge. At the age of ten, she had had read "The Last Days of Pompeii" by Lord Lytton, encouraged by her schoolmistress. 'Well done,' she said. 'Read it again when you are older.' I am not too sure what it was all about but I certainly read every word. *Precocious brat*, she thought.

Back to Roget and having moved on from retrospection to reflection the trail then led to pensiveness, quiet, thoughtful. At one point, she came across the name Wilhelm Wundt. 'Never heard of him. Let's look him up,' she said to Fluff; 'learn something new.' With no yowls or objections, she turned to Wikipedia, a slightly dubious source of knowledge. Wilhelm Wundt, philosopher (1832–1920) states that the source of personal knowledge is subjective, not possible in animals or children.

Then, considered Alexa, at what age are you no longer a child and become aware of personal knowledge? A few words further on she alighted on introspection, examination of one's feelings and motivation. 'This is it, Fluff,' as she gave the cat a bear hug.

I don't know if a psychiatrist would agree but I have been trying to explain my thoughts, my attitude to life and introspection seems to fit the bill.

Another large mug of tea for Alexa, a few cat biscuits for Fluff and some sideways thoughts and she was already halfway into inheritance, desperately trying to remember the double helix, a former subject she had delved into with enthusiasm at one time and not understood too well.

'Right,' she said out loud, 'let's see what I can remember.'

The double helix is composed of two curved ladders that intertwine. The letters AT and GC make up the rungs. A will only pair with T and G with C.

Sugars make up the handrails. The two ladders unwind to form a complimentary partner which is a template to create a new double helix.

Oh dear, she thought. 'Have I got that right? It's a long time since I attended a chemistry lesson. I'll try to look at in a simpler way. I am made up of half my mother and half my father; that bit is simple. Mother was a kindly lady of kindly parents who helped people wherever she could, so hopefully I have inherited some of her traits. Father was less nice but had come of a family who had suffered through hard times echoing back to the Potato Famine so perhaps my less nice character comes from that side.'

'There is some good in the worst of us,' wrote Martin Luther King, 'and some evil in the best of us'; his version of a well-known quote and surely, he experienced more "evil" than most.

Thinking back, Father loved animals which is in his favour. During the war my parents invited a husband and wife whose house had been destroyed in a bombing raid to share our home which they did for four years.

So hopefully I get my kinder side from both parents; my desire to help everybody from my mother's side and my desire to know and understand everything from my father.

'Enough,' she announced to Fluff. This latest quest was prompted by thoughts of Roisin. 'I must put her out of my mind. But I do wonder how she is and what happened to her,' she said wistfully.

Chapter 11

Millions in Ireland had died from hunger, disease or emigrated in an attempt to start a new life.

Official births and deaths records almost disappeared, even in towns or cities. Decades later in the villages and surrounding countryside of Belfast, as life returned to a semblance of normal, records were pieced together from old letters, tenant leases, army records and memories handed down from the survivors, the difficulties compounded for the Kellys by the fact that the eldest son in the Kelly household was always christened James.

In Ballycona, an isolated population, hardly a village, more a hamlet, records were scant and not too accurate to say the least. The first World War impinged greatly on the country with many men sent to fight though the struggle for survival still remained the primary problem, the daily fight to find enough food to keep body and soul together.

So it was surmised by the descendants that Samuel, the younger brother of James, had died along with his wife and all his children.

Samuel's land was sold off to the landlords and the small amount of money it raised went to elder brother James, now an unhappy, middle-aged widower undecided about any future left to him.

A diligent minister of the local church searching for records of the nineteenth and twentieth century found that a James Kelly of Ballycona married Elizabeth Cameron in 1895 and produced twelve children. Further enquiries revealed that every week he went to market and spent half of any money he had made on drink on the way home. Rolling into the cottage he would have his wicked way of the uncomplaining Elizabeth who produced child after child until she was exhausted and eventually died.

This brood was a clever lot who, as soon as they were old enough, moved from home and made lives for themselves. One went to Scotland and became a chemist at the Nobel factory and later died in the huge explosion that took place there in 1914.

One of the girls who had a beautiful singing voice, began her career in a music hall show, then went on to join an opera company in the north of England. Another emigrated to Canada, bought himself a piece of land and raised cattle. Samuel, a teacher at the local school, the spoilt baby of the family volunteered to join the army in the first World War and was killed on his second day on active service in France.

The current James, as the eldest son, found himself inheriting the cottage and the small amount of land in Ireland and feeling rueful and resentful that the others in the family were able to escape and start a new life while he was left with this small inheritance, barely giving him enough to survive.

One evening while sitting in front of a meagre peat fire James reviewed his assets; a broken down cottage, three small plots of land in poor state and still not recovered from that terrible day when the potato disease was first discovered, a young son, of course named James, and a young daughter conceived late in the marriage, whose mother died shortly afterwards leaving James with another "asset", much loved and named Roisin.

A short distance from the cottage lived a kindly, late middle-aged lady called Grace, the only survivor of her family. In return for a small amount of food, she submerged her sorrow in looking after James's cottage and his two young children. She had cared for the old folks until they "had shuffled off their mortal coil". Frankly it was a relief to have two less people to find food for. Hunger had almost certainly contributed to their deaths.

Weary to the bone, the current James felt he no longer had the physical or mental strength to carry on. He sat up all night figuring out how he could create some sort of life for himself and two remaining children.

By the early hours of the morning, James had made his decision. He would leave Ireland, leave Ballycona and try his luck in England. He did not tell the children.

He would sell the cottage and the three small plots. With the money raised and the small amount left to him from Samuel, he would convert the farm cart into a caravan, harness up the two old horses and with the milk cow attached to the back and make his way to England; the chickens would have to be left behind, He would make his way to Belfast docks and thence to Liverpool. God knows what awaited him there, but it surely could be no worse than what the family had gone through in Ireland.

He decided to ask Grace if she wanted to accompany them, conscious of how little he had to offer but she accepted immediately. 'You are the only family I have left. Who would look after the children?' she replied.

'God bless you, Grace,' said James trying to hide the tears. 'We will share whatever we have with you.'

It took several months; the first, most important job, was to create a frame on the cart and cover it with a canvas and tarpaulin roof. A curtain separated off a small sleeping area with bunkbeds for James the elder and his young son and another for Grace and Roisin. As much of the household goods as possible were packed into the remaining space, the seats becoming beds at night for Grace and Roisin. Cooking would be carried out over an open fire or paraffin heater outside the caravan.

Conditions were nigh on impossible. James had read enough books to know the saying, 'Packed like sardines in a tin.' This was the reality, but decisions had been made and now there was no alternative, no turning back.

On a late spring morning, James checked the newly made caravan for the umpteenth time and with Grace and the children on board, he took a final look at the old homestead. This done, he drove the old horses, Whalebone and Clearway, with the cow tethered behind out on the road to a new and uncertain future.

He drove the horses very slowly; they had a long way to go, and James stopped every couple of miles to give them a rest. The children thought it a huge adventure not realising the travails yet to come.

By evening, as the light faded, James pulled over on to a wide verge, unharnessed the horses and allowed them to graze. Grace put together a meal for the foursome and after clearing up they all crawled into their bunks for a few hours' sleep. It was far from first class accommodation but at least it was dry and warm.

James was woken by someone shouting. He scrambled out of bed to find an irate man banging on the door.

'Bloody gypos! Get off my land. Who the hell do you think you are?'

Feeling this was not the time to argue and telling Grace and the children to stay in the van, James silently harnessed up the horses and moved off down the road as quickly as possible. So this was a foretaste of things to come. No doubt there would be insults aplenty.

They were now on the edge of Belfast so after a meagre breakfast, Grace milked the cow and they continued on their way. James's plan was to get through the city before the traffic built up and make their way down to the docks and get a boat across to England.

They both heard and saw the docks long before they reached them. Steam vessels had replaced the sailing ships and the noise, steam and workforce had massively increased since around the 1800s. James stood at the entrance to the docks and watched the scene below. Men trying to urge their reluctant horses on, others screaming at them to get out of the way. Steam, smoke, the blasting of horns from the ships, thousands of men surging around like ants conjured a scene akin to "Dante's Inferno". Creeping through the city with a reluctant cow in tow had been a masterclass in patience and navigation. He suddenly felt exhausted and short-tempered.

Eventually, James crossed the yard and leaving Grace and two frightened children in the caravan forced his way to the office to pay for the passage to England.

'I want to get to Liverpool the cheapest way possible.'

Peering through the dirty window the man behind the desk started shouting, 'Bloody Hell, what do you think this is, a travelling circus?' as he took in two horses, a van and a cow tied on behind. 'This might cost you a bit more.'

Suddenly, James saw red and lost his temper. *I've paid over the top already.* The months of decision, tension, hard work suddenly got to him. How dare this plump, well fed rogue sitting in his nice warm office try to make a bit extra for himself?

'You may force other people to grease your palm but not me,' screamed James, really wound up now, continuing, 'no doubt your family made a packet out of the famine. Well, mine didn't. So we are going to England to try to make a living to feed the kids, the horses and the cow. OK. So. Do I pay the proper price or make a visit to the harbourmaster to tell him what you are doing?'

'Go on. You tell him,' shouted the queue of men, egging him on, lining up behind. 'He's been cheating us for yonks.'

'I wonder what the authorities would think about all the extra cash you make. Shall we ask them?' shouted James.

'Alright, keep your hair on, mate. We had it hard, too you know.'

'Not as hard as we did, I assure you.'

'Look. I'm sorry.' He hesitated. 'Go to the far end of the dock. You'll find the steamships there. They should take you. Here's your tickets; and I wish you luck.'

Knowing he was on a loser he spoke quietly and politely, more out of fear of being reported for cheating than behaving in a civilised manner. His face had gone pale and his hands were shaking.

Calming down, James led the two horses and the cow across the dockyard to where the steam ships were hissing and hooting. Whalebone and Clearway were spooked and resisted crossing the planks on to the boat, nearly sending the lot of them overboard. In the van Grace, James and Roisin cuddled one another for comfort as upset as the horses. Eventually the animals were got on board, tethered to the rail and with much shouting and blowing off steam they set sail across the Irish sea. Unable to resist, James turned and watched as the coastline of his homeland faded from view. 'Will I ever see this land again? Do I want to?' he muttered. He turned his face towards England and the hope of a better life to come.

The Irish sea gave its usual vengeful crossing, with huge waves crashing over the deck, flinging the boat from side to side and soaking the green-faced passengers most of whom lay around groaning and vomiting in misery.

In the early morning, the sea calmed down as they sailed into Liverpool docks, thankful to be alive. *At this moment, I don't think I want to see my homeland again*, thought James. *I never want another journey like that.* But his main priority was to get the animals ashore and tend to Grace, James and Roisin all of whom looked tired, ill and in need of food and care.

As in Belfast, James eventually led the frightened horses and the cow off the boat and made his way, as quickly as possible, out of the dockyard and on to a street, still noisy and crowded but a bit more peaceful than that terrible, rocking boat. Looking up at the sun he estimated his way south and set off through the grimy streets. His aim was to get through the city and on to the minor roads as quickly as possible.

There were not too many people abroad; night workers coming home, others setting out for a day's labour. The cow tethered to the back of the van caused a lot of ribald remarks and amusement; cars being more the norm these days. James manfully drove on until they, at last, reached an area where the houses were more scattered, with surrounding gardens and there was a view of green fields beyond.

James reined in the horses, jumped down and led the animals onto the wide green verge. Having had their heavy leather collars removed Whalebone and Clearway eagerly began cropping the grass. The cow eagerly joined in on the feast.

'Grace. Can you get us something to eat? Are you feeling well enough?' called out James poking his head in the van.

'I'll milk the cow first,' she replied as a man yelling his head off came running in their direction.

'Get on your way!' he bawled, running up and shaking his fists. 'We don't want gypsies here.'

James, exhausted almost beyond thinking, faced his opponent.

In a quiet manner, he politely asked the man if they could stay one night. 'We have just come off the boat. I have an elderly lady and two young children with me; they need food and rest. I give you my word we will not leave any rubbish behind us. Please.'

The man's attitude suddenly softened. 'One night,' he said. 'We have had a lot of trouble with people leaving piles of rubbish behind them. I've had my own problems in the past. Do you want water? I see you've got the milk sorted.' He laughed. 'I bet you had fun getting that through Liverpool. Come on, bring your can,' as he made his way back down the lane, James following.

Having filled the can at an outside tap he was about to go when the man came over and handed him a small box containing four eggs.

'Off you go and don't be there in the morning. I'm trusting you now. You look a bit different to the others.'

'Thanks. We'll leave it tidy, I promise.' *Well, England is not so bad*, he thought. One good day's start thought James; it was not to last. They would face hostility, hate and at times violence as they progressed southwards but meantime eggs, bread and milk for breakfast.

Guided by the sun, James moved on southwards and now westwards always wondering where he would find a permanent place to live. He felt a terrible responsibility for Grace, young James and his daughter. He had done his best for them, taking them out of the grinding poverty of Ballycona but had he brought them to anything better? He would lie awake in his bunk every night young James sleeping beside him, wondering if he would ever find a permanent home for them.

So far James had been able to pick up a day's work here and there, on the farms or road mending for the local Council. He was a good worker and probably could have stayed longer but Grace and Roisin bore the brunt of the insults and possible violence all day so they had to keep moving, James always making sure his temporary site was cleared up before he left.

What had the tenant farmers of Ireland done to get to this state? Life was already at existence point with most of the population almost at starvation level. He came to the conclusion that the awful Potato Famine was primarily responsible, recalling the day when he found his crops turned to mush, the effects of which had compounded the existing situation of poor soil and was still affecting them decades later. The government and the greedy landowners did little to help people at the time and were not doing much more now. All he could do was to keep travelling and pray and even God didn't seem to be listening. They now travelled more to the west and for weeks skirting the towns of Liverpool, Birmingham, Stroud, Glastonbury, on and, on always sticking to minor roads and in the evening turning down narrow lanes in search of somewhere to stay the night.

After many days, when the sign Okehampton showed up James veered away from the town, moving into the closed down, secretive part of central Devon. It was a difficult procedure as they had to cross a main road. One very early morning, before the traffic of the day built up, and with Grace acting as a look out, James led the horses, van and cow across the road. Only one vehicle came along and slowed down, the driver looking hugely amused at the cavalcade, waved to them and smiled. The children waved back and then they were safely across. As soon as he could James turned down a minor road. They had moved into a different world, an enclosed, silent place.

Here the soil was a deep red, fertile, with grasslands on which to graze and fatten cattle. The noise of gurgling streams could be heard and the water sometimes ran down to the road; a land where the trees almost met overhead and smaller lanes led off often ending in deep combes shielded by younger trees. Sometimes there was an isolated farm at the end of the lane where the farmers kept sheep and cattle, letting them roam free and graze on the rough area that led up to the moor. What a lonely life they led, in isolation, cut off from the outside world in a house that had been in the family for centuries.

James got down from the van and began to explore. When he pushed through the bushes and found the stream, he tasted it; the water was clear, sweet and fit for drinking. There was little traffic in the lane, a farmer taking crops to the local market and occasionally a flock of sheep blocking the road driven along with the help of dogs. If James could park out of sight, he could walk back to a village shop to buy potatoes, bread and a small amount of bacon to give a bit of flavour to their very basic meals. He could purchase grain and fodder for the horses and the cow mindful that they were totally dependent on these animals who had to be kept in good condition.

They drove on through small hamlets, just a few scattered farmhouses; young children playing in the gardens, a housewife hanging out the washing. Beyond this the area grew more isolated and with the sound of a stream gurgling in the background James decided this was a safe place to park. He quickly led the horses and cow through the trees and out of sight. Once they were parked and safe, the harness removed and the animals tethered and allowed to graze, Grace took the children out foraging for mushrooms, herbs and anything green that could be cooked and added to the potatoes that mostly had to be bought from a village shop.

Occasionally, a farmer would allow them to walk a field and pick up any potatoes left after harvesting. James was desperately holding on to the money from the sale of the homestead and plots in Ireland in the hope that one day he could buy a small area anywhere, to create a home for Grace and the children. He carried the money with him sewn down in a pocket to protect it from thieves.

James now began to feel a little more relaxed, a little more secure. They met fewer people, so less insults. Providing they were moving on the local people seemed friendly.

One evening when he was taking a rest on his own in the bunk which he had to share with young James at night, he heard the faint clip-clop of horse's hoofs. Jumping down from the van he spied a small caravan pulled by a single horse coming down the lane. The driver pulled up and stared warily at James. 'We're not doing any harm,' he called out. 'Leave us alone.'

It had been such a long time since he had met another traveller that James ran to meet him. 'No, no. It's alright. I am pleased to see you. Are you on your own?'

Seeing that James appeared friendly, the man jumped down and came over.

'My wife and child are with me. My name is Fred. We are travelling south to try and find a permanent place to stay, but no luck. No one will have us. All we get is abuse and told to move on. I don't know what will happen to us.'

Eager to talk to another man, James said, 'Let's sit on the bank and share stories. It's good to talk to someone in the same boat.' So the two men swapped their news and misfortunes for a few hours.

'I thought it might be better over herein England,' volunteered Fred, 'but it's not. I suppose you don't see the poverty and hunger that we saw back in Ireland but where are we going to live? We can't just keep roaming the roads forever.'

'I am hoping a farmer or someone will let us stay on the moor. There is a vast area of empty land available. I looked it up on the map; it's called Dartmoor. We could make ourselves self-sufficient. I am sure we could; we have the necessary knowhow.'

After a few hours, as the light faded and the night air grew cold, James turned to Fred. 'Why don't we stick together?' he said. 'There will be more protection with the two of us. We can share whatever food we have, the women and children will have company during the day and we will feel happier leaving them when we are out looking for work. Grace is teaching my two to read and write and I am sure she wouldn't mind teaching your little girl as well.'

'That sounds like a good idea. I would certainly be happier leaving Stella, my wife, knowing that Grace is alongside her.'

James felt a lot easier in his mind. Though it was now dark the two men sat talking, planning, formulating ideas. Life suddenly seemed a little better to have someone to share in the daily fight for survival.

By the early hours of the morning, now half frozen, they had decided on a plan of action. James went back to his van and climbing in beside young James who, fast asleep, didn't even feel his father cuddling up to him for warmth. Eventually James dozed off knowing that though nothing much had improved, at least he had someone to talk to and share the problems.

In the morning, the horses were harnessed to their respective vans and with the ever faithful cow in tow the two families set off, always towards the moor with the hope that they make a permanent home there. They were now gradually travelling west in Devon with Cornwall beyond.

After a meagre breakfast, James and Fred set out to find work of some sort. They didn't care what it was so long as it brought in a few pounds. Fruit picking, general work on a farm, sometimes building or repairing roads for the local Council, they could feed the women and children.

Almost hidden down the narrow lanes Grace and Stella got on well. Grace taught Maggie, Fred's daughter, young James and Roisin basic reading, writing and arithmetic. Grace was not so much clever as able and back in Ballycona where she had attended the local school, the schoolmaster recognising a bright mind, had encouraged her in her studies and had hopes she might get a job, perhaps in a shop, even as a clerk in an office, and escape the dull poverty of home. Alas, young Grace was pulled out of school to look after the old folks until they died. Now middle-aged, she had missed out on marriage and lived in solitude in a broken-down cottage on her own until James asked her if she would help to care for his children when his wife died. She became a different person and taught and cared for the two young ones almost as though they were her own. She passed on anything she had learned at school and then took them into the woods and fields to collect mushrooms, herbs and plants.

Roisin could milk a cow, feed chickens, not that there was much to feed them on, make and mend clothes at an early age, turning her into a useful person which would help her so much in the life that was to come. Now, a natural earth mother, Grace was going out in the early morning and letting the three children run and play for a while. They were the better for it. Their pale faces began to acquire a bit of colour, they had more energy. Hope was in the hearts of all of them.

Chapter 12

When work for the men ran out, they moved on, always sticking to the closed in lanes and pushing into the trees at night.

Life went on this way until they came to a signpost pointing to the Dartmoor National Park. Here lay the hopes of James to find a piece of land where they would be allowed to stay. They drove along the edge of the moor until the land sloped upwards a clump of trees with a small area of grassland just beyond, big enough for the two vans, the horses and the cow to be hidden from passersby going along the bottom road. Waiting until the light was fading James and Fred encouraged the animals uphill and installed them behind the trees.

Thankfully, they stayed the night without interference and in the morning James and Fred, after telling Grace and Stella to keep close to the vans and avoid attracting any attention to themselves, discussed their plans. They decided to walk to the nearest village and try to gauge the view of the locals on caravans parking on the moor. Going into a tourist centre, they looked around at maps and other walking gear they pretended to be interested in.

'Can I help you?' enquired a polite young man.

'We are interested in the moor. We know very little about it,' replied James.

'I can show you some good guidebooks and maps if that would help.'

'Well. You must know it well. Tell us about it.'

'I can't help noticing your lovely accent. Are you from Ireland? Am I right?'

'Yes. We are on holiday,' he lied. 'And just having a look around the country. It's a beautiful place here.'

'Yes, it is but it can be a dangerous place with its vast, bare areas, bogs and rivers. Many a walker has got lost and we have had to send out a search party to find them, usually hungry, very cold and frightened. You know the story of "The Hound of the Baskervilles". It's not as bad as that but needs to be taken seriously. It is best to avoid the north end of the moor. There is a government firing range on that part. It is further into the moor but severely fenced off, so there is no real danger but best to give it a miss. Walkers usually enter the moor further south to get onto the more popular trails and pathways.'

Not knowing the Sherlock Holmes tale, James enquired naively, 'Are you allowed to camp on the moor?'

'No; it would be too dangerous, rain and sudden mists that come down quickly, you get disorientated and anyway there are no facilities for camping. You are not allowed to light a fire as it could spread quickly and destroy ferns and plants. We want to keep it as a natural wild place, a place of beauty with sheep, cattle and, of course, the famous Dartmoor wild ponies.'

'You obviously know a great deal about the moor. Thank you for telling us about it and I promise we will be careful and not get lost. You have been very helpful.'

'You are welcome.'

'Goodbye.' And when completely out of earshot, 'That was more helpful than that young man realised,' said James. 'Allowable or not, he has just told us the best place to hide out and set ourselves up.'

'The north end of the moor where few people go, not even the rangers it seems and just below the firing range,' replied Fred.

The two men walked back to their current hidey hole with smiles on their faces and a feeling of optimism.

Grace, Stella and the children were playing a board game in Fred's van as there was more room there. They looked at the smiles on the faces of the men.

'Why are you looking so pleased with yourselves?' asked Grace.

'I am not going to raise your hopes,' replied James, 'but maybe we have found somewhere to live. It will mean a lot of work on the part of all of us. Just don't say a word to anybody for the time being.'

'Is it allowed?' asked Grace. 'I mean, will the Dartmoor authorities actually let us stay there permanently?'

'Probably not,' replied James, 'but as the leader of this small group I am prepared to take the risk.'

'I will go wherever you take us. You have looked after us so far. I put my trust in you.'

James once again felt the huge responsibility for looking after Grace and the children. Their faith in him was touching. He would not fail them. Two apparent hikers, in the early morning, striding through the nearby village caused no concern to the villagers; they were used to seeing people setting out for a good walk.

James and Fred, each with a stout stick cut from the hedgerow, were on a different mission. Their aim was to find a place where the two families could live a quiet life, be self-sufficient and not be constantly abused and shouted at. They would deal with their rubbish and obey the laws of the moor as far as it was possible. They just wanted peace.

Beyond the village the lane became narrow. Every so often the trees thinned out a little with the beginnings of a narrow roadway leading off in the direction of the moor. Investigating these they found that some just dwindled out, others were too narrow to allow the horses and vans to get through. One, though, looked promising. About half a mile from the village, an opening around twenty feet wide, eventually leading out to an area of grassland sheltered by half grown trees. The road grew firmer underfoot with pieces of rock strewn across it and an area ahead and slightly lower, probably a quarter of a mile away was clearly the workings of an old quarry.

James felt a frisson of excitement, his heart pumping, his breathing faster.

Could this be a possibility?

The quarry workings had left a pit and at the top of the rise on the far side stood a half collapsed stone house or workshop. James's thoughts were leaping ahead. This was building material. The two men climbed round the side of the pit and up to the house and found themselves looking out over miles and miles of bleak, fern covered land. For a moment, he imagined he was back looking across the bogs of Ireland. A slight mist hung over the moor. In the far distance, something was moving. Half closing his eyes a group of something could just be seen; the famous Dartmoor ponies.

Booms and bangs were a reminder that the firing range was not too far away. Walkers did not visit this part of the moor. The rangers had enough to do in the more popular parts, so this area was left alone, somewhat neglected, ideal for a hideaway.

To the right of the quarry, down a slope, was a combe; a deep thicket of trees, below the grassy area they had first encountered. Climbing down to investigate they found a flat space, that with the removal of one or two small saplings, would leave them hidden from the world. In the distance, a stream gurgled on its way. Coming down from the moor the water would be clean and could be used for drinking, washing and supplies for the animals.

James turned to Fred and hugged him, a somewhat unusual gesture for him. There were tears in James's eyes and he brushed them away hurriedly.

'I think that if we handle this situation quietly and carefully, we have found ourselves a home,' he said. 'It will need a lot of careful planning but I believe we can do it.'

Night after night, James and Fred discussed their plan. The first thing to be done was to enclose the small field for the horses and the cow to graze on. The caravans could be parked behind the knot of trees. The final section would eventually be dug over to give an area where crops could be grown.

A few days later, armed with axes, a saw and a sledgehammer the men strode through the village as though as on a walk, their implements hidden under their coats and made their way to the gap in the trees and up on to the moor. There were plenty of branches lying about having been snapped off the trees in the wild winter gales. Their first task was to collect as many as they could. Cutting off the side shoots with the axes, the pile of wood grew. They worked like slaves all day and as the light faded, made their way back to Grace, Stella and the children for a meal of roadkill rabbit, potatoes and greens from the wood.

Both men were used to building fences on the smallholdings back in Ireland so that would not present a problem for them.

They set off before daybreak each morning with less chance of being seen by the villagers. They had decided that if questioned they would say they were rangers working on a fence to stop the ponies from straying on to the road.

As the first light filtered in James and Fred sorted out the strongest branches and began hammering them in at intervals around the area, leaving a gap for a gate which still had to be made, then began filling in the gaps with the smaller pieces, weaving them in and out to give strength. When the sun was high in the sky, they rested awhile to eat their bread and morsel of cheese, drank some water, then got back to work.

As the light faded James and Fred made their way back to their still hidden vans. Both of them were tired to the bone but satisfied with the work accomplished. In ordinary life, it would be time for a long soak in a hot bath but neither had that luxury and had to settle for a cold water wash and a dinner made of what Grace and Stella had managed to scrape together.

A gate roped on to the fence with an iron hoop at one end to close it had taken two days to make and install but now this was the first task completed.

They had not seen a human being so far which seemed to endorse the feeling that no one visited this area.

It was exhausting work but hope drove them on.

Two days had to be given over to finding local work. Following manhandling lumps of rock, fruit picking seemed like a holiday.

After much discussion, the men decided go a long way round, avoiding the village and come on to the lane higher up above the gap in the hedge. That way they would avoid being seen taking the same route every day and set people wondering what they were up to.

The next job was to investigate the combe to see what small trees had to be removed and to flatten out the land ready to build the first house.

Over the next week, a flat area well hidden by trees was established with a shallow slope leading downwards. Pieces of rock were man handled or rolled down the slope from the disused quarry to make a path and provide the foundations for building. This is the time they could have used the horses but decided against it.

The move from their present site had to be discussed like an army campaign and carried out quickly over one day. The plan was to get the horses and vans and the cow installed in the fenced off area behind the trees and then start building permanent dwellings.

One evening James sat on the steps of the van just thinking. It was a warm evening and he was enjoying a rare time of quiet and solitude.

Who am I? he thought. *What am I? Where am I going? Am I doing the right thing?*

I am a middle-aged man, survivor of a family who have lived and farmed in Northern Ireland for a couple of centuries. I have broken the tradition of the eldest son inheriting the cottage and land and brought my remaining family to England in the hope of a better life. Sometimes in my dreams I hear my ancestors cursing me. I pray for their understanding. I am someone who is going to break the law. What does that make me? A criminal?

As to where I am going; Only God and time will tell.

The night air was growing colder. He had been content in this hidden dell but knew it could not last. His prayers and speculations over, he got up from the steps and went into the van.

The Big Move, as they called it, started at daybreak. The children were detailed to pick up every piece of paper or rubbish within twenty yards of the vans. James was determined not to leave any trace of their having been there. They had been like cats with their toileting, taking a trowel and digging a hole, performing and then filling in the hole with soil. The trowel was cleaned with leaves and the leaves buried.

While Grace and Stella took the children into the woods to search for greens, James and Fred lashed down their belongings in the vans with rope to stop them sliding around as they made their way along the road up to the moor.

Having checked the site and with the women and children safely stowed on board, the men harnessed the horses and set off, James leading with Whalebone and Clearway, followed by Fred leading his horse Sunshine, some hundred yards behind with the cow in tow. They left the small cart used for visiting farm shows well hidden in the bushes to be collected later.

No one took any notice of them as they circuited the village and turned off into the small, dark lane overhung with trees. Back tracking, they found the gap in the hedge where James pushed, shoved and encouraged the two big horses and then Fred's pony up the slope onto the moor. There was something of a scare as a lorry passed by but the drivers waved their thanks as Fred pulled over to let them by. As quickly as possible, they got the smaller van off the road and out of view.

With a drink of water for horses and men, they let the women and children out with stern warnings not to make a noise and set off up the long slope to the fenced part they had prepared.

Once the vans were through the gate and hidden behind the belt of trees the horses were unharnessed and let free in the fenced off field. It was as though they had been let out of school. They skittered off, whinnying, kicking their feet in the air, even rolling on the turf. The cow greedily started to munch at the grass. James felt a tear coming and hastily wiped it away. He had not seen the animals behave like this since they had left the farm in Ireland. Once they were more settled he would build a shelter for them as it would turn bitterly cold In the winter.

But first they had to get through the night. It would seem they had accomplished the first part of the plan successfully. The adults spent a sleepless night waiting for rangers or the police to pounce on them, but no one came and they emerged tired but heartened by their first night of "freedom". Relieved, they set about the next phase along the rocky road and down into the combe.

James and Fred had decided that the basic requirement was for a more permanent base on which to build houses. Now high summer, their aim was to have some sort of habitable dwellings in place before the onset of winter.

Going up to the quarry, it seemed it would be easier to roll or push down lumps of stone into the combe below rather than try to manhandle them. They started with modest sized pieces, then went into the combe to dig an oblong trench filling it with irregular shaped pieces, infilling as they went and ending with flat stones that could be concreted in to form a floor.

All that heavy work was exhausting but each morning the two men started at daylight and gradually began to build up the sides leaving a gap for a door and a smaller space in which to fit a fireplace. Slowly the house began to grow. The walls were made of branches interspersed with straw and clay. The roof would be made of branches forming an archway, then laid over with planks, which they would probably have to buy, and topped with straw thatching.

After months of work, with days off to work on local farms and bring in some money, the house neared completion. Wherever they could, the men negotiated building materials in lieu of cash. The farmers were quite happy to exchange a pile of wood or an old iron stove for labour. They were not interested in where the goods would end up. They got a few days' work, cleared some of the rubbish lying around and most important of all paid no income tax. Everyone was happy, except the taxman, and what he didn't know could not upset him.

The building was somewhat unorthodox, a mixture of know-how from their days in Ireland and using whatever was available locally. The small rocks on the outside were filled in with wattle and daub, clay and straw, an age old method of making a building waterproof.

Though the vast majority of clay was on the south side of the moor, smaller deposits were scattered over all. A small amount removed from several patches, over a wide area, hopefully, was not as obvious as taking a large amount from one spot. Mixed with straw, or rough grass, this, slapped on the crevices between the rocks would give good insulation. The same mixture with more clay than straw on the inside and covered with planks where available would ensure warmth, much needed against the bitter winter they heard so much about. Two small windows gave a modicum of light; curtains drawn, a small log fire and a paraffin lamp lit in the evenings gave a cosy feeling and sufficient light for basic chores and reading.

James, concerned about the smoke from a peat fire, decided to use mostly logs and began collecting small branches and sawing up the larger ones, stockpiling for the dreaded season to come. A small amount of peat was collected from different areas, always making sure that the damage to the moor was minimal.

At last, the house was considered finished and Grace and the children helped make it into a home. A rug for the floor, blankets and pillows for the beds, a couple of which could be folded up in the daytime to give more room. Shelves and cupboards in one corner near the stove made for a cooking area. A drop down curtain over each bed conferred some privacy.

The great day came and the Kellys moved in. The contents of the van were quietly transferred and arranged by Grace with help from Stella. The van, and the horses, would stay in the fenced off field to graze in the summer with extra food in the winter.

James looked around with some satisfaction. He had provided his family with a home. Pray God they were not found.

Cooking was done outside on a griddle in a pit to minimise any smoke.

Next on the agenda was a house to be built for Fred, his wife and small child. James repaid his debt in the work he put into the new building. With a bit of experience behind them, things progressed fairly quickly and now the men had high hopes that that both families would be in a warm and comfortable house by winter. A stable also had to be built where the horses and cow could shelter from the cold.

A repeat performance on the building of Fred's house was accomplished as autumn phased in and Fred, Stella and Maggie moved into the combe. The two vans plus the lightweight cart which they would need to collect provisions from the farmers' markets would stay hidden in the upper field.

A rota of duties was worked out by the adults. The men would get work on the farms where they could, to bring in some cash. On slack days, work was started on the stable and storage area. A compost toilet needed to be built behind the houses. The women and children would fetch water daily from the stream and collect greenery and fungi from the woods around. Grace had an amazing knowledge of herbs which she passed on. Sorrel, chickweed and nettles could be used in place of cabbage. Young Hawthorn leaves and flower buds made a salad.

Garlic added flavour. Crab apples and elderflowers were the basis of a refreshing drink. So much could be harvested if you knew what was safe and where to look.

So far there had been no visitors. The booms and bangs from the firing range kept the walkers away, so hidden down in the combe they all relaxed a little though the possibility of rangers or officials was always on James's mind.

Winter closed in bringing bitter cold and rain and eventually in December snow fell.

The whole area seemed to go quiet. Though the deciduous trees lost their leaves, there were sufficient conifers to form a roof over the combe so that little snow penetrated to the ground beneath. When the thaw came, the snow melted and dripped through onto the houses below. The combe floor became muddy for a while and then dried up leaving it refreshed and heralding the spring with its carpet of wild flowers.

As the season moved on, the cooking was carried out indoors and the fire kept at a minimum to avoid smoke but enough to give sufficient for heating in the house.

One early morning James climbed to the top of the quarry and walked out onto the moor. The dawn was breaking, a pale sun shed its light across the snowy landscape.

A mist hovered, joining the land to the sky. It was unbelievably beautiful. He stood there a while just soaking in the atmosphere, recalling the vast tracts of land back in Ireland surrounding the cottage and farm. As always there was this longing for his homeland but fortified by the beauty of the day James made his way back from Heaven to earth to start the day's work.

There were times when the rain came down endlessly. The men worked on with the building, the women still went out to tend the vegetable patch; the children stayed indoors doing their homework set by Grace and playing games.

The water rushing off the moor and down the gap into the lane, quickly eliminated the wheel tracks and hoof marks disguising the route to the old quarry and the combe.

Gradually, the new life settled into a daily rhythm of chores, each member knowing their allotted task. There were always jobs to be done. Every day the faithful old cow had to be milked, food found for the next meal. The men built a wash house for people and clothes. At two-week intervals in the colder weather, water was heated, carried in buckets and emptied into a large, shallow tub. Women and children washed first followed by the men. Clothes were changed and the dirty ones stomped on in smaller containers and dried around the fire. In summer, the women took the clothes down to the river to be washed and hung them on bushes to dry. Temperature permitting, men and women in turn stripped off and washed themselves. In modern-day terms, it was primitive but they all kept clean. It was no worse than what they had done in Ireland.

The women and children had worked hard on the vegetable area and sometimes there were surplus crops to be sold at the farmers' markets held throughout the season.

On these days, James and Fred would load up the small cart with whatever they had to sell or exchange, harness up one of the horses and set off across the moor, being very careful to slip into the lane that led to the village without being seen.

At the market, a motley collection of stalls, sheep in pens, tethered cattle and ponies were bargained over.

James and Fred bartered and sold their goods but perhaps of more use was the chance to get to know the farmers. By casual acquaintance, they gradually built up a coterie of who could be trusted, not that they gave any clues as to where they had come from.

On some occasions, if money allowed, they treated themselves to a drink at the pub and got chatting to the locals. If they had a drink, they always took back sweets for the children and a small gift for Grace and Stella, perhaps a bar of scented soap.

Of late, James had considered adding another member to their group in the combe.

They had now lived there for nearly two years without being discovered. What if he or Fred became ill, how would they manage?

Of course, it had to be done carefully and secretly. He would need to pick the right person. He also had another reason.

For the last three visits to the pub, he had had his eye on a tall, strong-looking man, a bit of a loner, cleanly dressed, neatly cut beard. He rarely spoke to anyone beyond the publican. Thirty years old at a guess.

James moved over to the table where the man was sitting alone.

'Would you mind my sitting here?' he asked.

The man looked up surprised. 'No, no. You are welcome.'

'Bit crowded today.' He sat down and took a long swig of beer. 'I needed that. I'm James.'

'I'm Hugh.'

'Had a good day?' asked James.

'Just looking around. How did you do?'

'Sold some vegetables and got rid of some scrap iron I had salvaged from a local farm. Amazing what people will buy.'

'You live around here then?' enquired Hugh.

'Not too far away. What about you?' They were skirting around each other like players on a chessboard, both seeking information, neither giving anything away.

Hugh lifted his face up to James. 'I live where I can, work where I can and eat when I can.'

'Do you have any transport?'

'I have a pony and small cart. Why all the questions?'

James was quiet for a bit. 'You seem an honest chap to me. I am taking a chance. I think we can help each other. I could give you a place to live and grazing for your pony if you are prepared to help with the general work to keep us going. We are a very small group who are self-sufficient.' You must not say a word to anybody, the Dartmoor Executive would not be too pleased and the local Council would charge us tax if they found out. I have the feeling you would be pleased to stop the endless moving on and the constant insults. Believe me, I know. I have been through it. Think about it and we'll meet in the pub at the next farmers' market in a month's time.

James stood up. They shook hands and parted.

Collecting the horse and cart, he linked up with Fred, drove back through the village and quickly and quietly slipped through the hedge and onto the moor. It's like coming home, he thought as the old quarry came into view. It feels like home.

That night as James crawled into his "bedroom", the size of a broom cupboard, and pulled down the curtain; he took a minute to thank God for a safe home, shelter for his family and Fred who had turned out to be such a helpmate and friend.

He pulled the blanket over him and lay there thinking. His instinct, so far, about Hugh was that he appeared to be a loner, wanted a more permanent place to live and was a physically strong man. He could be an asset to the group and a friend for Roisin. She was growing into a beautiful young woman and would soon be casting around for male company.

If Hugh turned out be suitable and had the wish to live in the combe, James could encourage the friendship and eventual union with Roisin. Was this the right thing to do? This is what Indian parents did and in general the marriage survived. Roisin could not cope with the outside world; she had known no other life than that of their small community and he could not risk letting her into the world beyond it. If not, her husband Hugh could at least be her mentor.

Grace was growing old; Stella was frail, and he feared for the children. But again, the question. Did he have right to dictate Roisin's life? Eventually James fell asleep, the question unanswered.

Chapter 13

James discussed his proposition to include Hugh in the group with Fred who, quite reasonably said if he could meet Hugh and found him honest, it would be a good idea. They could do with the extra manpower and another male would be further protection for the women and children.

At the next farmers' market, James invited Hugh to join their group on the moor.

James knew he was taking a chance but one he was prepared to accept. He warned Hugh that it would be hard work. Hugh could live in James's house until one for him could be built in the combe.

'I am just grateful to have the chance to live with you. I am so tired of the endless travelling,' said Hugh.

Having outlined their mode of living James drove his cart out into the lanes followed at a distance by Hugh's. James, after looking around, slipped into the entry to the moor. A short time later Hugh followed. He gazed with interest at the fenced off field where a couple of horses and a cow were contentedly munching grass. James motioned to Hugh to drive up to the belt of trees and called out to him to park his cart, unharness the horse and let him loose in the paddock to enjoy the grass.

With all the animals in and after carefully shutting the gate, James led Hugh down the now reinforced road to the quarry. Beyond lay the moor, green and lush, stretching into the distance. A couple of rabbits scampered by; ponies could be seen converging with the mist on the horizon.

Hugh gazed in wonder at the great open space then followed James and Fred down and into the combe.

'Did you do all this yourselves?' his eyes wandering over the houses and viewing the bathhouse. ''Tis a wonder.'

'It was also incredibly hard work which you will be expected to take part in and not breathe a word to anyone.'

Dartmoor

Dartmoor pony

'Gladly,' replied Hugh. 'I'll work as hard as I can for the opportunity to have somewhere to stay.'

'You can live in our house for now and we will get started on your house as soon as we can. Grace will feed you on what we have or can catch but contribute anything you have.'

Hugh fitted in well and next day started gathering the stones and rolling or carrying them down to the combe for the foundation of his house.

In between their work on collecting wood and doing the heavy work on the vegetable area, James and Fred helped and advised Hugh on the house. It grew steadily and within a few months the basic structure was finished. Grace, Stella and the children carried the contents of Hugh's few belongings into the combe and set about organising the living space. With a few cushions and blankets which he could pick up cheaply at the next farmers' market, Hugh would have a cosy and comfortable place to live.

One day when no one else was around, he got down on his knees and thanked God for these kind people who had taken him in.

Hugh was a kindly, honest man who worked hard, helped make stables for the animals, played with the children and generally fitted in, turning his hand to whatever was needed. James and Fred were relieved that their judgement of the character of Hugh had proved correct.

With Hugh settled into his house the work of the group settled into a routine, each member, even the children, having a specific chore.

Work began at first light with the men feeding the animals and working on the vegetable area. Roisin took a bucket and went down to milk the cow. Stella's girl, Maggie, was now becoming proficient at this and sometimes took her turn. The cow who had served them so well through all their travails was getting old, her milk yield growing less all the time and becoming insufficient for the increasing members of the group. James did not have the heart to sell off the faithful old animal to the slaughterhouse which in practical and financial terms he should have done. For the sake of the children, he decided to let her graze throughout the spring and summer months not giving her regular extra feed but let her live out her life in modest comfort. She would still be given a place in the barn in winter and minimum extra feed. She deserved that. A sentimental gesture on James's part he could not really afford. He would have to buy another cow.

Young James's job was to collect the water from the stream below the combe. Running down from the moor and falling over rocks to create a small waterfall was the easiest and cleanest place to do this. Hugh had bartered for a couple of milk churns and built a small hand cart which made life easier rather than struggling up the slope with buckets.

Meanwhile, Grace and Stella were preparing breakfast. Irish soda bread with a scratch of home-made butter and a cup of milk would keep the men going until they returned for a drink and another hunk of bread at mid-day. They met up at James's house for the main meal in the evening. The small field just beyond the vegetable area was given over to wheat. When ripe, the grain was coarsely ground into flour and the remaining straw dried to patch up the roofs of the houses and saved for winter feed for the animals. A short sleep and as dawn turned to day, they all went back to James's house where Grace provided breakfast, and took a brief rest.

The work to keep them self-sufficient was endless. There was always wood to collect for repairing fences, to be cut into logs for the fires in winter, laying up turnips and potatoes in the old-fashioned way of trenching them in heaps of soil.

No one complained; they were too grateful for somewhere to live. Everyone worked quietly, only talking to one another, if necessary, ever conscious of possible rangers climbing up or the military personnel coming down. The children were allowed to play, mostly when it was nearly dark, and instructed to keep the noise down.

One balmy, warm evening after the evening meal James sat on the log bench outside his house relishing the peace and quiet, the children in bed, Maggie and Grace resting.

He was content but how long would it last? This was the thought that ran constantly through his mind.

Fred came and sat beside James joined a while later by Hugh. The three men just sat there taking in the peace of their surroundings.

James suddenly got up, went into his house and came back with a sixpack of beer. Handing a can to the other two and taking one for himself, he opened and drank deeply.

'What are we celebrating?' asked Fred. 'We don't usually have spare cash for luxuries.'

'It's not a celebration,' came the reply. 'I thought we deserved it, the hard work, the constant worry.'

'I'll drink to that,' said Hugh, 'and thanks to you for taking us on.'

They all sat there in the cool evening air lost in their thoughts.

'I think it might be sensible if only one of us goes to the farmers' market,' said James. 'We could take it in turns to go and take anything for sale and pick up basic supplies. One horse and cart won't draw attention, three might.'

The other two nodded their heads in agreement. 'That makes sense to me,' answered Fred.

'And me,' said Hugh. 'Have you noticed there are far more cars than carts these days but not for us. Horses don't need petrol. Do you ever think about Ireland, about home and how we came to be here?' asked Hugh.

James, roused from his reverie, suddenly stirred. 'I think it is more why we are here rather than how.'

'Tell us then if it is not too painful.'

'My mother was a long suffering lady gradually worn down with all the childbearing. I was born way down the line of numerous children, always slaving away from an early age, never having enough to eat and watching the older folks gradually die off from hunger and disease. My elder brothers and sisters got out, moved on, some to countries abroad. I attended the local school; the schoolmaster did his best but the pupils always had to go back to the family and the farm.'

'My mother was a kindly lady, worn down with the constant childbearing and surprisingly lived to a great age despite illness and hunger. Every farmers' market day, my father went off to sell our meagre offerings. Calling in the pub on the way home he spent most of the money he had made and arrived home roaring drunk to create yet another child. I dreaded those nights. A curtain separated our bedroom part from the daily living space, and I would lie there sharing a bed with two others and try not to hear the grunting and screeching from the other end of the cottage.

'Eventually, my father would fall asleep, and snore very loudly. In the quieter pauses, I would hear my mother sobbing into her pillow. We kids tried to sleep, some of us not understanding all that had been going on. In the morning, with a thick head, Father would grab some milk and bread and totter out to start the day's work.'

'As my siblings moved on it fell to me as the eldest son left to try and produce some crops to live on and for sale.'

'Were you not tempted to move out yourself?' asked Fred in a quiet voice.

'No, there was really no choice. It was not all the old man's fault. The land never really recovered from the potato disease, the Great Famine, and didn't yield a good crop of anything. So I stayed on nursing the parents until they died. Then my wife died and I felt like following her but there were young James and Roisin to bring up so I struggled on until I couldn't stand it any longer and made my way to England. And I thank God daily for what we have. I miss the views of the land, how green it was and the people, those who are left. Ireland will always be my home but I cannot live there.'

'Ireland never recovered from the Great Hunger; the effects went down the generations and in parts is still affecting the land.'

There was a total, awkward silence. James sat staring straight ahead, can of beer in hand. Was he recalling the awful times or trying to suppress them? Eventually, he looked up and smiled.

'I'm sorry for your loss, all of your losses,' said Fred.

'So am I,' followed Hugh.

'My story is no worse than millions of others,' replied James. 'This was meant to be a sociable meeting. Tell us about your life, Fred, then you Hugh so it is all out in the open and we can put it behind us.'

'Well,' started Fred, 'I suppose my life was one of poverty, hunger, watching family and cattle die. Like yours James, our bit of land never recovered. I was always hungry. I thought to try my luck in England. With the few pounds, I got for the cottage I bought a pony and van; at least I had somewhere for my wife and children to live. I took the ferry across, made my way down south and thank God met you, James. I am content. I pray it lasts.' He looked across at Hugh. 'Your turn.'

'I don't remember my parents. I just recall sleeping in barns or in the fields, and like Fred, always hungry. I did go to the local school where I learned to read and write but clerical jobs were not available for the likes of me. I really only went to school to get some food. The schoolmaster and his lovely kind wife sort of looked after me, gave me food when the others undid their kerchiefs containing bread, sometimes an egg so I could eat with the others. We were given a small cup of milk. When my schooltime was over, I lived on my wits for a while, then made my way to the Belfast docks, stowed away and found myself in Liverpool.'

'The surprise was that everyone seemed to be as badly off as me. I worked and ate when I could. I managed to barter for a very small amount, an old cart and an aged horse. The farmer was kind and let me patch up the cart in return for some work. I slept in his barn at night. Eventually I set off on the road hiding in amongst the trees at night, sleeping under a tarpaulin, working where I could. I would do anything to keep me and the horse going, road working, clearing drains just anything. Then one day I found myself at the farmers' market and you know the rest.'

The three men sat silently for a while.

James stood, addressing the other two, 'We will not speak of this again. Agreed?'

Fred and Hugh nodded. 'How long have we lived here? About eight years. The years roll by. I have three more cans of beer. Let us drink to good fortune and go to bed content.'

Chapter 14

Back in Hertfordshire, Alexa was reviewing her life. Retirement was growing ever nearer, and she had decisions to make. She loved her job, the excitement of discovering something new, the quiet satisfaction of solving the cause of a patient's bleeding or clotting problem. Haemostasis had been a somewhat not fully understood subject for many years but with modern techniques becoming available many more answers to the problems had become available.

With clever and cooperative staff helping, the group were able to pin down a diagnosis and then hand on the work to the molecular scientists for further investigation. The resolving of DNA and the double helix had opened up a whole new world.

At home, cats had lived and died. Each death meant more tears and another place in the pet cemetery at the end of the garden. The present incumbent was a tortie with white shirt and socks rescued from the gutter. A spoilt but lovable animal she was fussy about her food, slept on Alexa's bed every night and, of course, went to Cornwall twice a year.

Alexa still visited Robert's posh shop in the village, going to Tesco's in Falmouth for the rest. She handed over a few paintings to Davey, the landlord, who took them away to get a good sale price, the money to go to the Penzance Lifeboat Fund. She shared an occasional drink with Tom Banham and laughed about the astonishment of the lady that they had been discussing pilchards and not having an affair. She had even been invited to give a talk and show some slides of her trips to the Gambia. Such kind, goodhearted people who had little but gave so much. She loved them. How she looked forward to moving down to Cornwall permanently.

Mrs Nicholls, her neighbour, aging quietly, sustained by the whisky and other goodies Alexa had brought back for her still looked after Erin, the new cat, when she had to spend a night away from home.

'Do you mind, Mrs Nicholls? It has been such a help to me to know my pet is being looked after.'

'I have loved them all, dear. One worry I have is when you will retire from work. I know you intend moving to Cornwall permanently.' The old lady started to cry. 'I shall miss you and the pets so much.'

'Firstly, retirement is a few years off. Then you can come down for holidays. I can get someone to put you on the train and I will pick you up at the other end in Falmouth. It is so beautiful, and you can stay as long as you like. You could move down there if you wish; there is plenty of room for you in the cottage. I should love to have you.'

Mrs Nicholls cheered up perceptibly. 'Could I really live down there?'

'Of course. I mean it. You've got a few years to think it over. Let's have a cup of tea and there are some of those Cornish biscuits left.'

The day took on a better prospect for both of them. Teatime over the two women got on with life feeling much happier.

Alexa lived what some called a solitary life.

'I am so sorry for you,' said one, 'living on your own, no husband or children.'

Sally, her best friend, whom she had been sat next to first day at the Grammar school had remained her best friend through the years. They had laughed and cried with one another and best of all shared their secrets and not revealed them.

Sally had three children by a hard drinking, gambler husband. She loved the children dearly but on occasions could have done without the husband.

'I am going to leave him. I can't stand his gambling and drinking any longer,' she confided to Alexa one evening.

'I would,' she replied, 'but I don't have three kids and no money. You have to talk to him. Tell him how you feel.'

'I am a trained florist. I could work.' She took an intake of breath. 'Sometimes I envy you.'

'Life has not always been honey for me, you know that.'

'No. I know but you now have the freedom to do what you want.'

Alexa felt desperately sorry for Sally. Following the death of her husband at a young age, Alexa had never felt the need to marry again. She had had a few relationships, some enjoyable for a while but they all fizzled out by mutual agreement. The final one, Angus, was extremely clever, handsome, wealthy; he seemed to have everything. Then she learned that his wife had walked out on him and she began to wonder why. He visited her more frequently always expecting a meal to be ready for him and sex to follow.

Alexa was a good cook, a competent housekeeper and provided the sex Angus demanded. When he said, 'Marry me,' just that, after a particularly satisfying meal and too much wine on his part (Alexa was a non-drinker), she suddenly realised that what he wanted was somebody to look after him and his house. There had been no romantic build-up; no 'Darling I love you. Will you marry me?'

Furthermore, he had informed her that he couldn't cope with a cat and had donated his family moggie to the local research institute. That was it. She did not wish to be a servant, she had her own very interesting job and she was petrified that her own beloved cat would join his.

He got up and walked out and that was the end of a questionable relationship.

Am I too harsh, too demanding? Is it my fault? She worried about it for a while then decided she preferred a cat to a man and had lived a contented life since then.

Sally did not have that choice but was canny enough to put down a deposit on a florist's business which flourished due to her high standard of work. With the help of her mother who coped with the children, she eventually paid off the mortgage. The ironic part was that her husband lost his job and ended up working for Sally and was dispatched at 4 a.m. to the flower market in London every morning. The marriage survived; just.

Chapter 15

Time and the seasons moved on.

Winter on Dartmoor is cold. In November come the first frosts, covering the grass and coating the rocky outcrops. A heavy mist often hangs over the moor and by December the snow starts to fall; sometimes a few inches but can reach several feet. The ponies grow shaggy thick coats and push their muzzles through the snow to get at the grass underneath.

Some of them would come to the edge of the quarry staring hopefully for food.

James the elder would occasionally take out a bundle of hay though the group could barely afford it but he could not bear to see the animals looking so hungry. Survive they did, as they have done over the centuries.

The horses and cows in the small paddock were overwintered in the stables built for them by the men. Given a small amount of oats and hay each day they were warm and sheltered from the harsh weather. On the days that the sun shone, James let them out to get some exercise and push through the snow to get at the grass beneath. They were better cared for than many, certainly those back in Ireland. These animals were vital to the existence of the group in the combe and needed to be kept as healthy as possible.

Then came the first stirrings of spring. The weather grew a little warmer. The snow melted, grass started to show green again, most of it having turned brown due to the harsh winter. Primroses, sweet scented violets began to appear; then the light green of the leaves on the trees. Dartmoor was a magical place in the spring. The ponies frisked, birds started to build their nests and birdsong was heard again.

Now the real work began. Up at first light vegetables and corn were planted. The women and children worked alongside the men from dawn to dusk. Grace still found time to give lessons to the children, simple arithmetic, reading and spelling but mostly about cooking and what plants from the moor could be eaten.

Herbs were gathered and dried for flavouring the food but mostly to be made into medicines as they had no access to doctors.

Their whole lives were centred on survival but however hard the work, no one ever complained; they were too thankful to escape from the endless travelling, the abuse, the hunger.

In summer, the sky became light early with sunrise streaking the heavens, swathes of apricot, orange and blue. The moor was now shades of green. Surplus crops were taken to market and basic necessities purchased. Only one man went to the market; they took it in turn to minimise the risk of being seen coming off the moor. The men worked on the local farms or did any casual work available to bring in a little money which went into the communal fund always being careful never to reveal where they lived. Cash in hand suited the contractor and the worker.

On one such day, on a bright morning, it was the turn of James to visit the farmers' market. He and the pony trotted happily along the lanes enjoying the summer warmth and turned into the field where the market was being held. There were more cars and lorries these days than horse drawn carts but still a place was set aside for them. James chose a position on the edge of the area; gave the horse a drink then fixed the nosebag filled with hay over the animal's nose. He spread out the vegetables over the back of the cart and soon sold the lot.

Taking a wander around the field to find the stall selling cups of tea, his eye was drawn to a young woman sitting on a log with a small boy at her side. Getting closer James could see that the young woman was thin, poorly dressed and she had been crying, the tears still running down her face.

Although he had never read the book, it could have been an enactment of Thomas Hardy's "The Mayor of Casterbridge"; another Susan Henchard awaiting her fate. A poor analogy as the child beside her appeared to be a boy. Though the days of selling your wife had gone, this young woman clearly needed help.

Distressed to see it but cautious of being accused of bothering her, he called out, 'Would you like a cup of tea?'

She looked up at him and nodded; the child clung more closely to her.

James went over to the stall and bought two cups of tea, a cup of lemonade and two buns. The boy grabbed his share and gobbled up the food and drink as though he hadn't seen food for a while which he probably hadn't. The young lady ate the bun and drank the tea slowly as though savouring each mouthful. 'Thank you,' she murmured.

'I shan't hurt you,' said James drinking his mug of tea, 'I have a daughter and son of my own.' He bent towards her. 'What are you doing here?'

She looked up. 'I have nowhere to go,' she said and started to cry again.

'Where have you been living?'

'The boy and I sleep under a cover, an old tarpaulin, in the woods. In the daytime, we come out onto the roads where people sometimes throw us food. I don't know what is going to happen to us.'

'Who left you there?'

'A cruel man who hit me. Today he found us, brought me and my boy to the market then left us here.'

James stood looking down, something forming in his brain. He thought of his wife, his parents, his friends who had all died from hunger and illness and in that moment his mind was made up.

'I can offer you a place to sleep, a little food but you will have to share in the work. Do not speak of this to anybody. We have to trust each other.'

'I will do anything to keep my child alive.'

'Can I trust you?' asked James.

'I promise. Just help us, please.'

What would the others on the moor say? More mouths to feed, another sleeping place to find. But he could not walk away from these two.

'Wait here while I make my purchases and I will come back for you. Follow me at a distance to where the horses and carts are, then wait and I will call you when I am ready.' He repeated again, 'I shall not hurt you.'

James, having completed his shopping, walked back past the woman and motioned to her and the boy to follow then assisted the pair to climb onto the cart and covered them with sacks.

They must trust me, he thought. *Or they wouldn't submit to being treated like this.*

Untying the tether from the tree, he jumped up on the front of the cart, set the horse at a trot and made his way back down the lanes and on to the moor.

Hugh was waiting in the paddock, ready to unload the goods and got the shock of his life to find a woman and young boy lurking under the sacks.

'What the hell?' he exclaimed.

'Get them off the cart and go and get Grace,' shouted James. 'Yes. I know they are there. Go on, quickly.'

Well. He's the master. Who am I to argue? thought Hugh and ran off up the hill to find Grace who was resting in James's house in the combe. 'James wants you now, in the paddock.'

'Why? What's the matter. Is there trouble?'

'I don't know what's going on. You had better come and see. Come on.' He helped the increasingly arthritic lady from her chair and up to the paddock.

'Ah Grace,' said James. 'We have visitors. Would you kindly find them something to eat and a place to sleep for the night?'

'Yes, of course,' replied a bewildered Grace. 'Come with me.'

The mother and son clung to one another in fright. Grace went over to them and stretched out a hand to each of them. 'It's alright. You will be safe with us.' Cautiously they stepped forward and the three of them walked down into the house in the combe.

After a helping of rabbit and squirrel stew, Grace put a blanket and pillow on the floor and motioned the pair to lie down. Covered with another blanket they almost immediately fell deeply asleep from exhaustion.

'Who are they? Where have they come from?' asked Roisin staring at the sleeping forms on the floor.

'I don't know,' said Grace. 'They clearly needed help and your father is looking after them as he looks after us all. And don't make that face, Missy. You were without a proper home for a long time so go to bed and say your prayers. Don't forget to thank God for all you have and that you have a kind father.'

Oh God, thought Grace. *More mouths to feed but we shall manage somehow and learn a little more in the morning.*

Down in the paddock, James called Hugh over. 'Now that you have a house, your van is only being for storage. Right?'

Hugh nodded wondering where this was leading.

'This mother and boy desperately need a home. Would you move the contents of your van to the stables so that the pair can live in there after we have all made it clean and homely for them?'

'Of course, James. I am so lucky to have a house. Whatever has happened, I am sure they need a home.'

'Thank you. I will get everybody together later and explain the situation.'

'James. You are a good man,' said Fred. 'We will make them welcome.'

Early the following morning, before the day's chores started, James called everyone together except the new girl and her son. He addressed the group, 'At the farmers' market yesterday, I came across a young lady clearly in great distress. She had a young boy with her and when I spoke to her, she said she had nowhere to go. I realise that we cannot take on the world's homeless people, but this young woman touched my heart. I trust you will treat her with kindness. Grace, would you fetch them to meet us, please?'

Grace went to James's house and with one on each side brought them to meet her new friends. They were thin, dirty and desperately shy.

'Welcome to our group,' said James. 'Life is kindly here but strict. You must follow our rules; do you understand? and you and your boy must help with the chores. Hugh has given over his van for you to live in. Grace and Roisin will help you to settle in. You will eat with the rest of us. We are hidden from the world out here on the moor and it must remain so.' Turning to Grace. 'Give them a bath and find some clean clothes for them. You start work tomorrow. Don't be afraid. You are welcome here.'

Each member of the group came over to the young lady and shook her hand which started her crying again.

'What is your name?' said Roisin.

'I am called Siobhan.'

'What a pretty name.'

She smiled for the first time. 'And my boy is Connor. Thank you for letting us stay. I shall work hard and not let you down.'

'Tomorrow, you work. Now, let the rest of us get on,' said James as Grace led the mother and child away to get cleaned up.

Grace looked at the pair and thought. *You need a good bath; you are filthy*. She set a large bucket of water on the stove in the van to heat up and led them out to the bathhouse. 'Take off all your clothes, you and the boy.' Siobhan crossed her arms in front of her and just stood there. 'I can't get you clean with your clothes on. Now take them off. Nobody can see you.' Reluctantly, the pair undressed, Siobhan retreating to the corner of the shed and trying to hide.

'They have probably got lice,' muttered Grace and went off to get the herbal antiseptic.

When the water was hot Grace tipped it into the bath, added another of cold and told Siobhan to step in. Grace was quite shocked at the state of her; she was thin, really dirty and had many sore patches on her skin besides the bruises inflicted by the violent husband. *Poor child*, thought Grace, all her mothering instincts to the fore.

After the layers of dirt had been washed off and covered in ointment, Siobhan put on underclothes, a skirt and jumper that had belonged to Roisin.

'There, that's better,' said Grace and started on the boy who was even dirtier than his mother. Washed and dressed in some clothes formerly belonging to young James, he looked a different child. 'Now for your hair,' and standing back to avoid the black creatures in their hair leaping on to her, she applied her lice killer then washed their hair with soap.

'All done,' said Grace. 'You can spend the night here while Hugh is removing his goods and then move into his van tomorrow. We can find you a kettle and some covers to start with and you can add to it bit by bit.' Grace thought of the stall at the farmers' market where she could pick up a few bits for very little.

'Why are you crying?' asked Grace as Siobhan held her head in her hands and wept.

'You are all so kind to me. I am not used to it.'

'We do not have much but what we do have, we share. But you are expected to work and help with the daily chores. Everybody is kind and no one will hurt you. Now I have to get a meal ready which we will all share. Would you like to help me?' Like having a daughter, another child she had never had. The two women sat together and washed potatoes and cut up greens and an animal which had already been skinned. 'Please James, don't bring any more waifs and strays home,' she pleaded quietly.

'Where does the meat come from?' asked Siobhan.

'One of the men goes down to the road every morning and picks up any roadkill. The men shoot rabbits but there are so many of those it doesn't seem to make any difference. There are just as many the next year.'

Each one had their own thoughts about where they lived and their style of living.

James the elder daily thanked God for the place they had found and lived in for so many years. He had brought these people here and felt it his duty to safeguard their lives as much as he could. They had survived hunger in the early years, illness; living without medical care, relying on Grace to get them through with her herbal medicine and salves. Education of the children. They knew the ways of the countryside, could do their sums and read and write but how they would fare in the big wide world was a constant worry. He had to train a man to be the leader of the group in case something happened to him. Roisin had grown into a clever and beautiful looking girl. Perhaps he could marry her off to Hugh. *I shall think about that one. I don't know how either of them would feel about it.* He was not getting any younger; he had to get things settled. Every day he worried that they would be discovered. The responsibility weighed heavily upon him.

Grace, who had taken her chance and come to England with James, had no regrets. Now ten years older, stiff and arthritic, life was still better here than her lonely, miserable existence in Ireland. She was able to pay by contributing her knowledge of edible plants and herbal medicines. Above all was her love for the children. She had taught and continued to teach them all she knew to fit them for a world beyond Dartmoor; this life could not go on forever. One day they would be discovered and who knew what would happen to them then. Meanwhile she carried out her duties with care and thanksgiving for the life she had.

Fred just got on with his daily chores, saying little, grateful for a place for his wife and child to live. He didn't think where he would go if they were found because he didn't want to know. For the time being, he was content and ever grateful to James for giving his family this chance. His poorly wife, Stella, who did what she could was cared for with the help of Grace. Fred had had some schooling in Ireland; be it basic. He had men friends. Life for the moment was satisfactory.

Hugh was a loner. Having lost his family to hunger and illness he had made his way to England, always travelling south then west in the hope that it would be better than the north.

Providence sent Hugh to the farmers' market on the day that James decided he needed extra help. He willingly took part in the work schedule and played with the children. On occasions, the men he now counted as friends met on an evening when the work was finished and yarned about Ireland, nostalgia more prevalent than actuality. Hugh asked for no more.

The children Roisin, young James and Maggie were too young to know any other life and accepted their current situation as the norm. They did not realise how fortunate they were to have so much freedom, to run across the moor, swim in the river. In years to come, they would relish this time and remember it with pleasure.

Siobhan and her young son Connor were still somewhat bemused by their change of circumstances. Cleaned up, a change of clothing, food and somewhere to sleep was almost too much to take in.

In a matter of weeks, mother and son became different people; lively, realising that they would no longer get beaten and starved. There was a God she decided. She had asked for his help, and He had provided it in the form of James. They were grateful.

So, all of them were content in their differing ways. James constantly worried about his flock. The world was moving on and as much as he wished it otherwise, he was realistic enough to recognise that one day visitors would come and life as they knew it would end. What then?

Chapter 16

The village below the moor, a collection of old stone-built cottages along with an ancient church, had remained virtually unchanged for centuries. Most of the younger fraternity had moved away to the towns in search of work so the age range of those left was at the pensionable level. The old folk tended their gardens, visited the local shop which was just about hanging on, played whist weekly in the church hall and a few of them went to church on Sunday making it viable, just, for the priest to maintain a living.

A conscientious old man he visited his flock, tending to their needs as he was able, though almost in the state of needing care himself.

This quiet little community lived contentedly until the local Council announced that a Council Estate was to be built alongside the village to help with the ever increasing population. Then the fur started to fly. Meetings were organised within the local community. It was not, they pointed out to each other, that they did not want the sort of people who lived in Council houses next to them but the wildlife would be upset, the bees would no longer have enough wild flowers and someone was sure they had seen slow worms on their allotment which are a protected species. They took their comments to the Council who were not impressed. The arguments raged on for a couple of years but inevitably the project was voted through, the slow worms, if they existed, were given a new home on the moor and work began, as the villagers put it, on the desecration of the area. In truth, the village did not want to be disturbed. They just wanted their slow life to continue as it always had been but the times they were a changing and many more changes were about to come.

Around two years later, the building project was finished and families moved in, slightly bewildered by country ways but grateful for somewhere to live. The village shop was happy to have extra customers. The church even gained a few extra worshippers on Sunday, to the relief of the local priest.

A small gang of boys from the new estate gathered together and decided to explore the moor. Finding a way in, they followed the track along to the quarry.

James, alerted by the shouts of the boys, quickly sent word around for his flock to stay in their homes and out of sight.

Curious, as young boys are, they soon discovered the enclosed paddock with the stables and horses. 'I was told there was no one up here as it was close to the firing range,' said one.

'I shouldn't mind living up here,' another replied. 'It's nice, lots of fields to play in and no one to tell us off.'

They followed the path up to the firing range border fence with its big notices. Danger. No entry beyond this point. The sound of explosions came from further up. 'I think we had better go back; it seems a bit dangerous,' called out one of the more sensible, more frightened ones. So back they went the way they had come and did not visit for many months. James and his flock emerged from their houses and got on with living. They had not been discovered on this occasion but were aware that the outside world was encroaching.

The boys, a little older and a little bolder, decided to revisit the moor. Down through the quarry they scrabbled; then up to the firing range fence, pushing their way along the overgrown pathway which had become less obvious as time went by. It was still not a favourite trail for walkers.

There were no explosions or bangs today. A few tanks could be seen in the distance so deciding it was not exciting after all the boys made their way back down again and came face to face with James on his way to the stables.

'We weren't doing nothing wrong, Mister,' shouted one of the boys. 'Just having a look.'

'That's alright, lad. There's nothing much to see up there.'

'Do you work here?' asked one of the bolder ones. 'What do you do?'

'Keep an eye on the fences; make sure the ponies and the sheep don't stray on to the road.'

'Nice job. I'd like to work here one day.'

'Perhaps you will,' replied James. 'Off you go now. I have work to do.'

'Alright Mister. See yer.'

Safe again, thought James. *Harmless lads. Hope they don't talk.*

Life continued for the group. The lads found other things to investigate. Nicking fruit from the old peoples' gardens, smoking those new cigarettes that made you feel light headed that you could get from the men who hung around the pub. Life was much more exciting than scrabbling up the path to the firing range.

On an autumn evening, after a farmer's market, a group of men were drowning the day's work in a few pints of beer or cider in the nearby pub.

'There's some travellers or gypos whatever you call them living in the woods along the road that leads up to the moor,' remarked one.

'So long as they don't leave their rubbish behind, I don't mind. They have to live somewhere. Why don't the Council give 'em a bit of land?' said Billy holding up a pint pot and examining the contents.

'You go to church,' replied Sam, 'and believe that the thieving rogues wouldn't have the clothes off your back if they could. I hope your God can do something about it.'

They argued on putting away more pints. *A few too many*, thought Billy. *There'll be a few thick heads in the morning when the realisation came that they had drunk most of the profits from the farmers' market. Add in a few screeching female voices about how she was supposed to feed the children.*

James on one of his visits to the farmers' market took Grace with him. Not having left their home on the moor in a long time, she was excited; she had forgotten what the world was like beyond it. She dressed in her best clothes and climbed up beside James on the cart. On the back were the goods for sale and a wheelbarrow.

As they trotted their way along the lanes James explained the reason for the visit. 'There is a good jumble sale stall there and if I give you a few pounds, you could stock us up with winter clothing. It will look better a woman buying up ladies' things as well as men's. It might seem odd if I did it. Anyway, you know more of what everybody needs. Here is an extra few shillings.' He handed over a few paper notes for the main purchases. 'Buy something for yourself, Grace; you look after us all so well.' He suddenly stared ahead and flicked the reins at the pony, embarrassed at his speech.

'I am grateful for a home. I shall buy a bar of that lovely lavender soap you once brought back for us.'

James turned into the farmers' market, drove across the field and tethered the horse.

The scrap iron was soon sold as were the vegetables which always looked fresh.

He took Grace's arm and led her across to the jumble sale. Not quite as steady as she used to be, she was glad of a little assistance. 'I'll leave you here and go and get our provisions and come back for you. Are you alright on your own?'

'Yes, yes.' Grace was having a lovely time; she had not been away from the site for so long. The clothing stall was piled high and Grace, thinking of each member of the group in turn, methodically began collecting underwear, shirts, jumpers and outdoor coats.

'My. My,' said the lady behind the stall. 'You must have a large family.' She totted up the cost. 'The money we collect here goes to charity.'

'With a large family to care for, the mother can't afford to go to the shops, so they are grateful for it.'

'Well,' said the lady behind the stall. 'A little bit of money left. Go and get yourself a cup of tea. How are you going to carry this lot home? I hope you have someone to help you.'

'My son will help me. He'll bring a barrow.'

As if on cue, James, cap pulled well down to cover his face, appeared. With the clothes piled high, they struggled back to the cart and offloaded them.

'You've done well. You deserve a cup of tea and then you've got your own shopping to do,' said James.

At the tea stall, he bought two mugs of tea, an iced bun, and carried them to where Grace had found a chair.

'Have this and off to your shopping.' Tea drunk and bun eaten, Grace pottered off feeling rich with a few shillings in her pocket. She bought her lavender soap and then went back and got another one for Stella.

'Time to go home,' said James and off they trotted back along the lanes to the place they called home.

'I have had a lovely time,' said Grace turning her face up to James. He was such a good man, finding them a home, taking the responsibility of looking after them all. She recalled, as a young girl, being taken to Belfast and seeing all the shops, goods and clothing she had never seen before. Today had been as exciting.

'You will have a lovely time sorting that lot out when we get back.'

'I don't mind; it will all have to be washed. I'll get the girls to help.' She sat there looking around her, happy as Larry.

Next day Grace prepared the dinner early, then started on the washing. Roisin and Maggie, after milking the cow, had been given the day off from their usual chores to help.

The water heated, the clothes were soaked, rinsed and ready to be hung on the bushes to dry. Stella insisted on helping; she was touched and grateful for the lavender soap. They were all excited at the thought of new clothes; farmers' market jumble sale equating to Harrods in their world.

When all the washing was dry, it was folded (they didn't go as far as ironing) and sorted. The following evening, after the communal dinner, each person received a small pile of clean clothing which would see them through the winter.

The local boys, occupied with more exciting things to do, the group were left in peace and life went on peacefully for a couple of years.

One evening as a group of men from the village sat round a table in the pub drinking beer and idly chatting Sam remarked, 'Spring here again. I see them walkers are back. I can't see the sense of it, struggling up hills with packs on their backs. They can come and lump sacks of hay on my farm if they want exercise.'

'Oh, don't be such an old misery, Sam. If you lived in a smoky town, you'd be damned glad to get out on the moor for some fresh Devon air. Leave them alone.'

'Are those people still living up there?' enquired Daniel. 'My boy says he thought they had a right setup though he hasn't been up there for a couple of years. Bloke said he was a ranger.'

'Got better things to do, your boy, has he, like girls and drugs?'

'Here, mind what you are saying.'

Councillor Yeo, sitting nursing his pint, pricked up his ears at the thought of people living on the moor. It was illegal; it should be reported to the Council or the Dartmoor Association. He should look into this.

'You should take a look, Arthur. See what's going on,' said Dan.

The thought of more Council meetings, extra expenses, tickled Arthur's interest. 'I might just do that.'

'Shut tha' mouth, Dan. If there are people living up there, they are not doing any harm, or we would hear about it. Leave things alone.'

'But…' said Dan.

'I said leave it.' Though the thought of overweight Councillor Yeo struggling, gasping as he tried to climb up to the moor appealed to his sense of humour.

With the thought of extra expenses, on a fine day, Councillor Yeo parked his car in the layby where years before Roisin had appeared from the mist, picked up his water bottle, got out of the car and started up the hill. Gasping like a fish out of water and with his large, overweight abdomen preceding him he struggled a couple of hundred yards, sat down hurriedly, deciding it was not such a good idea and should perhaps be left to the younger fraternity.

Fortunately for James's group, the younger fraternity were not interested and in any case, the councillor was entering the moor in the wrong place, at least a mile from the encampment. He staggered down the hill considerably quicker than he had gone up, got into his car and decided he would stick to driving rather than walking or even consider losing a bit of weight. A couple of pints of beer less a week might do the trick. Still, the expenses from extra Council meetings would have come in handy.

So the group was safe for another couple of years and life went on as before. James's problems continued. Now a young woman, Roisin began to show interest in the opposite sex, her main focus being Connor who had grown into a tall, handsome lad.

In the evenings, after work and before dinner, the pair went for a walk along the river bank. Occasionally Connor would pull Roisin close to him and give her a friendly kiss. It was all so innocent; young love developing. James, not spying on them, just out for a stroll, witnessed this one evening and found himself with another problem to worry about. Connor was a young man with the normal urges of growing up; Roisin a vulnerable, almost childlike young woman. She had never had the guidance of a mother being still a baby when James's wife died.

So one afternoon he made his way to the house in the combe and found Grace resting after her morning's work. Surprised to see James at that time of day she sat up quickly and looked at him. 'Don't usually see you at this time of day. Whatever it is, it is better over a cup of tea.' She bustled around putting the kettle on the stove and setting out the cups.

'I just wanted a chat, your advice really.'

'I'll help if I can,' replied Grace. 'Do sit down.' She handed James a cup of tea and sat next to him, the only seating available.

'It's about Roisin.'

Grace looked at him questioningly. 'Yes?' she queried.

'She has never had a mother to talk to; been told things.'

Grace began to see where this was leading. 'You have done a wonderful job of bringing her up. She is a fine, beautiful young woman.'

'That is the problem. Does she know about grown-up things?'

'If you mean about periods? I told her all about that and I look after her each month, washing her pads, etc.'

'But does she know about babies and how they get here?' asked James wringing his hands and going red in the face. 'She and Connor go walking and I am frightened of what might happen. I feel I should stop her.'

'I shouldn't do that; it will only antagonise her. You talk to Connor, he's a nice lad, and I will talk to Roisin and I feel sure things will be alright.'

'I must get back to work,' said James. 'Thank you for your help, Grace. What would I do without you?'

That evening after talking to Siobhan who gratefully accepted James's offer of talking to Connor. 'He has never had a father who treated him like a normal boy, just shouted at him and hit him,' she said. 'After supper, I will visit Stella so you can talk to Connor here in the van. Thank you, James.'

Following the communal evening meal, Siobhan suggested that Connor go back to their van as James senior would call for a chat.

'What about?' asked Connor suspiciously. 'Have I done something wrong?'

'Of course not. He is a kindly man who has given us a home, so you be polite to him, please.'

Grace directed young James to Stella and Fred's van to play with Maggie for a while, so she had Roisin on her own.

'Right,' said Roisin. 'I am going out for a walk.'

'Not so fast, Missy. I want to have a chat with you.'

'What about?' in the same sharp manner in which Connor had replied to his mother.

'Sit down,' said Grace, 'and don't be so prickly.'

They both sat on the bed left as a sitting place during the day.

'You know about your periods every month, Roisin, but I want to explain what they are for.'

'They are a nuisance. I don't like them.'

'But they are a part of growing up. If a man and a woman put their private parts together, it can produce a baby. You and Connor go for walks and must be fond of one another. Has Connor ever shown you his private parts or you shown yours to him?'

Roisin's face went bright red, and she shouted back at Grace, 'No. You are horrible. Why are you telling me all this?'

Grace looked sadly at the girl before her. 'Usually, your mother would explain everything to you and Connor's father would explain it to him but neither of you have that luxury, so James and I are doing the next best thing. Don't be angry and upset, my dear. Your dad loves you and Connor's mother loves him.'

'My dad doesn't want me to walk with Connor; that it is what all this is about. He can't keep me to himself forever.' She walked across the van, flung herself on to her sleeping place and pulled the curtain down. Grace could hear the sounds of sobbing.

'Do you want a cup of tea?' Grace called across.

'No, I don't,' came the reply. 'Leave me alone.'

Best advice, thought Grace and got on with the pre bedtime chores.

Further up in the enclosed paddock, James senior knocked on the door of the van and called out. 'Can I come in?'

'Yes,' came back a frightened little voice.

James went in. 'Don't look scared. I just want a chat.'

'Are you going to send me and my mum away?'

'Good heavens no. You are both too helpful and too precious to us all for that.'

The boy looked relieved and sat there waiting.

'Did your dad ever talk to you about where babies come from?'

'No. He only ever shouted at me and hit me and wouldn't give us anything to eat. You and everybody are kind to us.'

James sat down. 'As you don't really have a dad, your mum has agreed that I should talk to you. Is that alright?'

Connor nodded. 'When young men and women grow up, changes take place in their bodies explained James. Young ladies have periods, they bleed a bit each month; it is quite normal and when young men get sexually excited they can give a girl a baby. Your mum and all who love you don't want that to happen until you are both grown up and able to cope with it. So, what I am saying is that you two must not put your private parts together or show them to one another. We only want the best for you.'

Connor still looking at the floor said, 'I am very fond of Roisin and would never hurt her.'

'I know you wouldn't. You don't even have friends of your own age to talk and joke with but you can always talk to me. Remember that you are a part of our family and that we all love you. Now off to bed with you; we have an early start in the morning. Bye Connor.' And off he went, back to his own house, feeling, at least, he had done his best.

Chapter 17

Grace woke early with the usual pain in her hips but warm and comfortable thought she would have a few extra minutes in bed. Eventually she stirred and muttering to herself, 'I have to get up and start,' pulled her curtain back, swung her legs round and plonked herself on to the floor. She dressed, then waddled across to the bucket of water in the kitchen, washed her face and hands and thought, *Right. Ready to face the day.* She opened the door and looked out up the combe. There was a distinct nip in the air. A mist hung over all and a light drizzle was coming down.

James had already left to start his chores, feed the animals, muck out the stable and increase the compost heap. He would return to the house later for his porridge. Young James was hanging about waiting for breakfast before he went down to the stream with Hugh to fill the water containers. There was no movement from Roisin's bedroom.

'Wake Roisin up, will you, James? Breakfast is ready,' Grace called out.

'She's not there,' shouted James. 'But she has left her coat behind.'

'Go and see if she has called for Maggie to start the milking,' replied Grace. James ran off to look for her.

Grace shut the door hurriedly to keep in the warmth. James burst in. 'She hasn't called there but Maggie said she will do the milking and take the ration round to each household.'

'Good boy,' she said and went to look behind Roisin's curtain. 'She hasn't taken her coat and it's cold and raining,' she said. Suddenly she felt a cold, sick feeling inside her. 'Go and find your father and ask him to come back home— NOW! Please.'

Young James ran off and Grace sat down hurriedly to stop the dizziness that had overcome her.

James senior came running in. 'What is the matter? Are you ill?'

'No, no. It's Roisin. I think she has run away. She hasn't done her jobs and her coat is still here and it's raining. I know she was upset that we spoke to her and Connor yesterday. She seemed to misunderstand us and started to shout that we would stop her being friends with Connor and now she is not here.'

James turned to his son. 'Go and get all the group here please.' Already his face had turned ashen grey, and he looked ten years older. 'I just wanted to help her Grace. To get her to understand about being grown up.'

'I know, I know.' Grace came over and put her hand on James's arm. 'We will find her; everybody will help.'

As the members of the group arrived, James addressed them, 'It would seem that Roisin may have run away; she was very upset yesterday. Can you help me to look for her?' His face crumpled for a moment then he pulled himself together.

'Fred, would you try the area where the lane leads on to the moor. Hugh, you take the path down to the stream with young James. You youngsters look in the stables or anywhere you can think of. I will try the quarry road that separates us from the moor, but I think the fence is too high for her to climb. Will Stella and Siobhan stay and help Grace with the dinner so there will be someone here when she returns. We will all meet up for supper as usual and swap details.' At the moment, it was "when she returns". As the days passed, it would change to "if she returns".

They all went about their duties. The rain was now coming down heavily. Roisin would be cold and wet.

Each house or van occupants prepared their own breakfast of coarse oats made into a porridge with the last of their daily milk ration then went out to start the day's work.

Grace would provide them with a hunk of bread and piece of cheese at dinnertime which would sustain them until the communal supper which was always eaten at James's house. Supper was usually a stew of greens and whatever animal, or bird was available at the time followed by a cup of tea. A substantial meal, it was a convivial affair like a family coming together. They talked, laughed and discussed for an hour or so then each one washed his or her bowl and returned to their own house or van. Most went straight to bed. One or two carved toys from sticks. And then to sleep, to face the coming day. Some, like James senior, read a book.

So, the situation turned full circle. As the group looked for Roisin, she was running down the hill not knowing where she was and almost colliding with

Alexa's car. As the men searched, Roisin was being looked after by Alexa and Philip, being integrated into the modern world, not stopping to think how much anguish she was causing.

After nearly a week when the search for a young woman had turned into the search for a body, when her dad grew thinner and would not, could not eat, Roisin decided to try and return home, back to the group.

Following along the moorland path, between Philip and Alexa, Roisin suddenly recognised the bush she had broken through on her way out, pushed her way past it and followed the noise of the gurgling stream, then ran up the hill and then down to the compound. Down to the house in the combe she ran, opened the door and fell into the arms of Grace.

'My darling girl. You are here, you are alive.' She hugged Roisin to her, crying onto her shoulder. 'Maggie,' she called, 'go and find big James and tell him Roisin has come home. Are you hungry? Here. Let me get you a cup of tea.' She released Roisin and set about bustling with the kettle and teacups.

Roisin was sat on the settee when members of the group came pushing into the house. Each one went over to her, took her hand and said they were pleased and grateful that she had been returned to them. Her father came last and just looked at her with tears running down his face.

'Welcome home,' he said.

Roisin looked up at him and saw how he had aged in such a short time and looked away. She felt deeply ashamed. She had caused so much heartache and not one of them had said a word against her. No recriminations; just thankfulness for her return.

'Let us all have a cup of tea then get back to work,' said James.

They drank their tea and Roisin was left alone with Grace.

'Do you want to tell me about it?' said Grace. 'You look well dressed and well fed.'

'What have I done to these good, kind people? Grace. Have I been horrid?'

Grace went over and sat next to her. 'Not horrid, just thoughtless. Now have a wash. Do you need to change your clothes?'

'No. I am quite clean,' as she lifted up her skirt and showed off her modern-style pants.

Shocked, Grace said, 'Who are these people who looked after you? They must have been kind to you.'

'Everybody was very kind. Alexa took me to her house by the sea and gave me food and a bedroom of my own to sleep in. She had two cats and they followed her around and then we went into a big town and bought clothes and saw a big patch of water and Alexa said the big boats went to the world to take things and bring them back.' She was gabbling and crying at the same time. 'And Philip, a policeman, helped bring me home.'

'Did you say thank you to these kind people?' asked Grace.

Roisin hung her head. 'No,' she said. 'I just ran away from them.'

'That was rude and ungrateful. Perhaps one day we will meet them, and you can thank them then. Now, have a rest. I have to get the dinner cooked.'

'No. I'll help you.' Grace produced a large haunch of meat and began to cut it up and put it in the pot.

'Where did you get that from?' asked Roisin in astonishment.

'Hugh found a young deer that had been killed on the road when he was out looking for you. It will give us food for a week. Call it a celebration dinner for your return.'

Dinner on the go, Grace unpacked Roisin's backpack. Emptying out the contents she picked up bras, pants, the new skirt and t-shirt, gasping in astonishment at all this new finery. She turned to Roisin. 'Did you like the outside world?'

'Some of it. The food and clothes shops were lovely and in the house, there was a thing called a television set and when you switched it on a picture came up showing places all over the world and people talking to one another. And there was an oven that didn't have a fire underneath. Alexa said it was heated by gas. Everything seemed so much easier, not the endless hard work we do here.'

'Did you want to stay in that world?' asked Grace.

Roisin looked down at the floor for a while then looked up at Grace. 'It was frightening at first but when I got used to it, life was so much easier and more comfortable. I thought I could live like that but after a few days, I missed you all and wanted to come home.' She started to cry. 'I'm sorry to have upset you all.'

'Now stop crying. It is over and nothing more will be said. Be nice to your dad. He deserves it.'

'I will. I will. He looks so old and ill, and it is my fault.'

'You can have the day off; tomorrow it's back to work. Now put these new fancy clothes away and help get the lunch ready; the workers will be in soon.'

Lunch was eaten in silence. Everyone smiled at Roisin, but nothing was said.

141

In the evening, when all of them gathered as usual for the evening meal, James motioned to everyone to be quiet. 'Let us say a prayer to give thanks for the return of Roisin to us. Dear God, we thank you for your mercy in giving us back our daughter, sister and friend. Amen.'

The episode was over; it would not be spoken of again. It had been a lesson to them all.

Roisin cried all through the excellent and unexpected venison stew. Thankful to be back, watched over with kindness by the other members of the group she continued her life on the moor, going on innocent walks with Connor.

Life returned to normal but a lesson had been learned. Never again would she behave like that. She had seen the effect it had had on all the members of the group, in particular her father.

It had shown that a maverick in the group could not be tolerated, perhaps a harsh word; allowable, acceptable would be better. The life on the moor was dependent on everyone doing their bit, playing their part, the whole workforce living as an interactive unit. Should one of them become ill then each person took on a little more work and gave some time to care for the sick person and worked a little later to make up for time lost. Everyone agreed with this and in turn gave or accepted the time and help of others.

The abandonment of everyone to search for a missing colleague was accepted by all but seriously interrupted the routine, the necessity to carry out the daily chores, to work with nature, not against it, to survive. Everyone had been greatly upset by the disappearance of Roisin and gladly gave their time to search for her, overjoyed and thankful for her return but it could not, must not happen again.

Next day after the evening meal when James had gone to check the site for the night, Roisin said to Grace, 'Why do we live here? Why don't we live in houses like the ones I saw in the world? I have never known anything else and have accepted it, but I don't understand it. I didn't run away because I don't like our way of life. I thought Dad wanted me to marry Hugh and not walk out with Connor.'

'Hugh doesn't want to marry you. He promised to look after you if your father for some reason couldn't do so.'

'Is my father ill?'

'No. He was looking to the future, just in case. One day I will tell you why we are here but enough for now. We all owe your father a huge debt of gratitude for the life he has given us. Now get up and help me. Do something, not just sit there asking questions.'

The seasons turned; the group had survived. James had become a little older, a little wiser. The toll of the latest episode had shown itself in the deterioration of his health. He could no longer manage the physical tasks as he used to and was thankful for the quiet, unobtrusive help of Hugh and Fred. He had to face it. He was getting on in years.

The men still took it in turns to visit a farmers' market to sell what they had and to buy basic supplies. James set out one morning in the pony and cart on his own. He wished to keep their profile as low as possible in view of the recent disappearance of Roisin with everyone searching for her, the men risking being seen as they had hunted beyond the confines of their establishment.

Having completed his tasks James took a look around and saw and heard some chickens squawking and scrabbling in a small enclosure. A cockerel strutted his stuff, showing off among the ladies giving an occasional cock a doodle doo.

James chatted to the lady in charge. 'Are they good layers?' he asked.

'Yes. They produce an egg a day, except him.' She pointed at the rooster. 'I expect he will end up on someone's Christmas table. I'd be worried if he laid an egg.'

James stood pondering the situation. He was soft-hearted and, after all the upset, thought that the youngsters deserved a treat.

'I'll have your four ladies if you have something to put them in.' He wouldn't take the rooster, nervous of him crowing in the early dawn and attracting unwanted attention.

The lady found a crate, money was exchanged and both parties were satisfied.

Arriving back on the moor, James summoned Hugh and Fred and asked them if they could make a run and small night shelter to protect the birds from foxes.

The chickens were let loose in their new home, given some corn, a bit of straw where they could lay their eggs and the youngsters were summoned. Up they came, Roisin, Maggie and young James and stared in delight.

'James has brought you a present,' said Fred, 'though I am not sure you deserve it, well, one of you doesn't.'

'Enough,' said James. Fred went quiet. 'I expect you to look after them, collect any eggs and share them with the others in turn,' said James.

Eyes alight with excitement, the youngsters agreed to the task.

Roisin went over to James. 'Thanks Dad,' she said.

After a while, there were a couple of eggs a day to collect and distributed with great pride in turn to the various households.

So the group once more survived and lived on as they had for many years. James continued to be their leader, the responsibility weighing more heavily as the years went by.

Chapter 18

Undoubtedly, the siting of the firing rage on Dartmoor plus the fortuitous discovery by James of the gap in the trees wide enough to drive in the vans and the ponies and carts to the road leading to the disused quarry and combe below allowed the travellers to set up home and remain undetected for so many years.

The firing range had been used as a practice site since the 1830s during the build up to the Crimean war. In those times, the moor was a wild, bleak place with few visitors or inhabitants. Cannons on wheels were manhandled or dragged up by horses with small risk of damage to the population. Rifles with blank ammunition were pitted against each other and if a few men got killed in the process by mistake then there were plenty more to take their place. No fences or warning notices were erected as visitors to the moor were virtually non-existent. Escaped prisoners from H.M. prison at Princetown, opened in 1809, were generally recaptured or shot before they reached the moor and those who did generally died of cold and hunger.

In 1869, one Henry Shrapnel developed a new type of munition and a place to put it into practice was needed. In 1875, an agreement was set up between the Duchy of Cornwall, who owned a great deal of the moor, and Okehampton Council. Flags were flown to delineate the area. The Okehampton Railway in 1871, facilitated the transport of large amounts of equipment on to the moor.

A considerable amount of the land was used during the first World War. During the second World War practically the whole area was requisitioned for storage and training.

The firing area at the north end of the moor was reduced in 1973 to around thirty two acres and has gradually been further reduced to twenty two acres with only one hundred and twenty days per year used for small arms practice.

The days of one man shooting another with a handgun or even with a wheeled cannon killing off several at a time have gone, giving way to computer controlled machines and the terrifying nuclear age.

After the end of the war, when walkers once more roamed the moor for pleasure, a number of the paths had become completely overgrown, in particular, the one leading up to the firing range. The only reasonable access was by the way in leading from the lower perimeter to the ancient stone circles to the west of the firing area. The large bush through which Roisin had pushed her way out to escape and back in was not an obvious route so by chance James had selected the most neglected and disused part of the moor at the north end.

Councillor Yeo played his part in keeping James's group safe though not quite in the way he had intended. The idea of giving up a few pints of cider a week and substituting salad for pasties followed by dessert with Devon cream seemed attainable and was for about two weeks.

Having retired from an office job, he had even less to do than sitting at his desk going through paperwork. He watched a lot of television during the day and his only exercise was tottering down to the pub in the evenings to meet up with his mates for a pint or two and a chat. The diet was boring and he was soon back on the pasties and cream.

'What are you having?' asked Dan.

'A pint of cider, ta.'

Then it was his turn to buy a round and then the others. He was soon back to five or six pints a night.

The pub was only about fifty yards from Councillor Yeo's house so quite easy to get to but one morning when he woke up feeling rather ill, the thought of walking to the surgery about a quarter of a mile down the road was a daunting prospect. After washing his face and dragging on some clothes, he went out to start the car. Trouble was that he had put on so much weight that the space between the seat and the steering wheel somehow seemed to have shrunk. He considered calling a taxi but what if he couldn't get in the car. How embarrassing. Should he ring Dan and ask him to come with his van? Same problem. Councillor Yeo was faced with the fact that if he wanted to see a doctor then he was going to have to walk to the surgery.

Heaving his bulk out of the door he set off. Past the pub he began to gasp for breath and had to take a rest. 'You alright, Mr Yeo?' asked a local lady.

'Just stopping for a little rest,' he called back. With frequent stops and feeling worse and worse, he finally fell in through the surgery door and collapsed on the floor his chest heaving, gasping like a fish.

The patients waiting their turn jumped up in shock. A receptionist came running over, took one look and shouted, 'Someone get a doctor out here.'

Dr Lakshar came running out stethoscope in hand and put it on to the old man's chest. His heart was pumping like a fire engine and the blood pressure monitor showed high, disastrous results.

'Call an ambulance and get the waiting patients into an empty room,' he demanded.

'Come along, ladies and gentlemen. Give the doctor some space,' called out the receptionist and shuttled the curious and frightened patients along out of sight of Councillor Yeo.

It seemed an age before the ambulance arrived. The driver and his co-worker, with the help of Dr Lakshar, finally managed to get the patient on to a trolley and into the ambulance. Councillor Yeo was no lightweight. With sirens screaming, they were on their way to the local hospital.

In Casualty, they went through a battery of tests and Councillor Yeo was admitted to the Inpatient Cardiac Unit.

Covered in wires and intravenous drips, Councillor Yeo survived a couple of days and then departed this life.

Mrs Woodham, who had "done" for him since his retirement, came to see him when he was in hospital, but he did not know her, so she went back to the house and waited. The news was not long in coming. Mrs Woodham cried for the kind, silly old man she had known for many years.

The news spread like wildfire through the village. He always had a cheery, 'Hello for everyone,' said one.

'And always drank too much,' said another.

'Not retired long,' they said.

He didn't appear to have any relatives, well, none who came to visit. No doubt they would appear if there was any money to be had.

'Who is going to arrange the funeral?' wondered Mrs Woodham. 'I'll talk to the vicar.'

Those like farmers who lived outside the village hadn't heard the news so when Sam went into the pub that evening. 'What's the matter with you?' Dan called out. 'Lost a quid and found fifty p.?'

'You haven't heard then?'

'Wot?' he said.

'Yeo's dead.'

'Dead. But he was in here a couple of days ago.'

'Happened quick. Had a heart attack; died in hospital.'

'Poor old Yeo. Always good for a laugh.'

The vicar arranged the funeral; the village folk turned out in force at the church and with greater enthusiasm at the wake in the local pub who had provided a good spread.

'Good turnout, Vicar,' said Dan. 'Silly old bugger. He was ill and wouldn't see a doctor. Oh, sorry. Didn't mean to swear.'

The vicar ignored the indiscretion, then after a pause, turned to Dan. 'He wasn't so much ill as lonely. I think we all failed him.'

They all looked somewhat shamefaced.

'Good day gentlemen. See you in church.'

'We should have helped him more,' said Dan.

They all felt a little mortal.

But the death of Councillor Yeo was a blessing in disguise for James's group on the moor who had never known of the intention to "shop" them to the Council. Life went on as the seasons turned; many had done so since James had taken the decision to get his family off the road.

Chapter 19

Back in Hertfordshire, retirement was growing ever nearer for Alexa. She enjoyed her job immensely, in particular working with the patients but the administration and staff problems were beginning to wear her down. She would be glad to go.

At home, she began to get rid of anything she felt she could live without ready for the big and final move to Cornwall. The charity shops did well and the binmen muttered about the extra rubbish.

It was then that a surprising letter arrived from Philip Warren, the policeman who had helped her return Roisin to her home on the moor.

He had been retired for some years and was enjoying life without the druggies and petty criminals. He had taken up walking again and sometimes drove back into Devon to visit Dartmoor. He had had no news of Roisin and her family so had to assume they were still there. They had remained hidden for many, many years now.

Did she remember Councillor Yeo? He was a nice man who had died recently.

The letter went on:

One day I dropped into the local for a pint and a sandwich and this man shared my table and started to chat. On hearing about my walk on the moor, he remarked that there were stories about a group who lived there, had been there for a long time but they didn't cause any trouble. I pricked up my ears wanting more.

His boy had met a man years ago, he told me, who said he was a ranger mending fences to keep the ponies off the road. Old Yeo heard of this, got a bee in his bonnet and was determined to find them but became ill and was never able to climb the hill to look for them.

And he is dead now so I suppose it will all die down again. They don't do no harm but I sometimes wonder about them and think they should be paying taxes like the rest of us. I might take a walk up there sometime to see what is going on.

And so might I, thought Philip. It is all so long ago. Roisin would be grown up by now. *Do you still intend to move down to Cornwall? Have you still got cats? Perhaps we could meet up for a coffee and talk about old times. I have a feeling that Roisin and her family will be exposed before long. So much more of Dartmoor is being opened up for tourists.*

Kind regards. Philip Warren

'Well. What a surprise; it must be at least ten years since we met,' thought Alexa. 'Amazing that the moor group have managed to remain hidden for all that time.'

Meanwhile, she retired from work. Not an auspicious ending to forty years' work. On her last day, she said goodbye, picked up a large bunch of flowers and a Waterford crystal vase and walked out for the last time. Of course, her favourite member of staff had written an anagram on the card which translated to something foul. Alexa was good at crosswords, so it wasn't a problem. She laughed and threw away the card.

No more getting the train at some unearthly hour into London to avoid the crush. No more being pressed against men's suits that should have gone to the cleaners a month ago. She got up and made a cup of tea and took it back to bed.

Fluff followed and having eaten a few cat biscuits settled down beside Alexa for a lie-in. They didn't stay long; there were exciting things to get on with. The house was sold, Cornwall awaited.

The days ahead were spent sorting the accumulation of documents, paintings not fit to be saved that had collected over the years. A couple of the lab staff had kindly offered to send on the contents of her office at the lab, so one morning a lorry arrived and delivered another load of paperwork and, it seemed to her, half of her laboratory as well.

There was again a vast amount of paperwork to be sorted but they had also sent syringes, pipettes and test tubes some of which should have been left behind but would be useful for future artwork. Most of it went to Ukraine.

Fluff "helped" by sitting in the middle of it and dear old Mrs Nicholls kept her supplied with constant cups of tea and homemade cake.

She had to keep reassuring Mrs Nicholls that she could come for a holiday and then decide whether she would move to Cornwall. Alexa had decided that if Mrs Nicholls cleaned up once a week and took a turn with the cooking, that would suffice on as rent. They would both have company and could share Fluff or rather Fluff could choose which lap she would sit on.

On the last evening, as she sat in the only armchair left, surrounded by tea chests and boxes, she began to think about her career, the funny incidents, the desperately sad ones. 'Let this be the cut-off point. Remember it then put the past behind you.'

She had started as a junior technician in a local hospital laboratory and was assigned to the histology department. Mr S. was a clever, noisy man who seemed to have deposited a good percentage of meals down his bright yellow waistcoat shouted at his staff, mostly at Alexa as she was new to the job. She was scared of him. This was as bad as school; she never seemed to do anything right.

Every morning she wrote the notes as dictated by the junior pathologist as he inspected, cut bits off the specimens from the operating theatre and transferred them to jars to be taken to the lab. She had always been a child with an enquiring mind so took the opportunity to look up in the medical dictionary any words, diagnoses, she had not met before. She learned a lot. Another task was to assist at post-mortems.

Mick, the technician in charge, on her first visit to the morgue laughed as he pulled today's victim out of the frig. 'Great advantage is,' he said, 'they don't talk back.' You needed a sense of humour to do that job.

Alexa looked at the white, warmed up body and thought, *I wonder what you would say. Have you had a good life?*

Dr Parker, the chief pathologist, a dour little man dressed in black jacket and pin-striped trousers looked a cross between a penguin and a lawyer from a Dickens novel. He had red hair and a sparse, gingery moustache. He stood there waiting to be gowned and gloved, then looked at Alexa. 'Have you seen a dead body before?'

'Only rabbits and birds,' she replied.

'Well, not much difference, but the humans are much bigger.'

And do not have big ears and a fluffy tail, thought Alexa. She was not in the least bit nervous, only curious. She had cut up and learned a great deal from the rabbits and "plucks", the heart and lungs still joined together, that Mother brought for the cat.

'Special, this one,' said Mick. 'Coroner wants a few bits.'

'Why?' from Alexa who suddenly realised she should have kept quiet.

'His doc thinks his wife might have done him in,' from Mick.

'Be a little more circumspect if you please,' said Dr Penguin. 'But we will need to collect a few extra samples.'

A piece of stomach went into a jar then several feet of intestine was pulled out and laid beside the body.

'Need a bucket for that,' muttered Mick.

For those not familiar with a post-mortem table, it has a slight slope downwards to a central drain to collect fluids and unwanted bits. When Dr Penguin had performed his duties, Mick manoeuvred the body to be ready for stitching up later, the length of gut, unnoticed, slowly and insidiously like a snake slithering through jungle undergrowth began to move towards the central drain.

'Oh my Gawd!' screeched Mick as the last of the snake disappeared down the hole.

Opening the door of the post-mortem at high speed, he rushed through and headed for the manhole outside. Hauling the lid off, he was just in time to see the colon slithering past. With a rugby tackle worthy of the Welsh squad, he made a desperate dive and just caught the end of it and hauled it back in triumph.

'Caught you, you bugger.' To the great the relief of Dr Penguin and himself, he finally trapped the beast and delivered it to the bucket. The good doctor, looking a whiter shade of pale, allowed himself to be ungloved and ungowned and left without a word.

Alexa, sitting in her chair, laughed out loud at the memory. 'My first and never to be forgotten post-mortem, Fluff. If we still have a kettle and a cup left, I need a cup of tea.'

The numerous sad memories she could barely think about. Several came to mind. Two, both little boys, both victims of the inherited condition haemophilia were stuck in her memory. Do not get involved, you are taught; remain unattached. Many will die; you cannot bear the weight of all that heartbreak.

Firstly Christopher, an angelic looking little boy, four years of age, whose small wounds seemed to take longer than most to heal up, had fallen off his tricycle and gouged his knee which refused to stop bleeding. A&E had referred him to Alexa for further investigation.

With the history taken, Alexa started the series of tests necessary for diagnosis. The boy, sitting on his mother's lap, whimpered as blood was taken for analysis.

'What do you think is the matter with him?' she asked. The poor lady was paler and more upset than the patient.

'We will have a better idea when we have carried out all the tests,' said Alexa gently. 'I am afraid some of them take a couple of days, but we will get them done as soon as possible then hand all the results to the haematologist.' Do not ever say, 'Don't worry,' she told herself and the staff, because she will and probably more so once a diagnosis is made. She made a polite goodbye to Christopher's mother, then handed over the tubes of blood for testing to begin.

Timothy had already been diagnosed as having haemophilia B. A noisy, difficult boy who had been diagnosed at birth was well aware that coming to her department meant that he would have needles stuck into him. For someone as sick he was extremely strong, resisting all on comers. But there was one trait she had become aware of over the years—Timothy was an ankle biter. His main target was Darren.

'Right, listen up please,' announced Alexa. 'Timothy is coming for a blood test so I shall need help. All please wear gloves.'

'Do I have to?' asked Darren; 'he's already got me once.'

'You can have a position away from the biting part. Let us form a plan of action. Aidan. We will sit Timothy on your lap. Cross your legs over his to hold them down.'

'Gina. Pull his right arm back and hold it firmly. Dougal, hold his head back firmly but kindly so as not to hurt him and stop him biting. Lisa: hold his left arm straight so that I can take the blood. As soon as I have the sample, press down hard to stop the bleeding. Lou, hand me the tubes, then assist Lisa to quickly strap on a dressing and everyone let go.'

'Anyone get bitten? OK. We know what to do next time.'

The mother kept apologising.

'He's frightened,' said Alexa. 'Just love him.'

Within the next few years, both little boys would be dead, victims of Hepatitis and HIV in infected blood which they needed to keep them alive.

Alexa sat in her lonely chair and felt the anger rise in her. She did not blame the government or the transfusion service for the infected blood. She did cast some of the blame on the commercial companies who, for profit, knowingly used it for treatment and diagnostic reagents. She recalled being shown an enormous, refrigerated room in Vienna with thousands of packs of blood or plasma brought in from South America hung up awaiting further use. There are clinics where the volunteers give blood for payment. 'The drug addicts will do anything to fund their addiction,' volunteered the young man showing her round.

'Not his fault. He probably didn't realise the harm strung up in plastic bags. He needed a job.'

In this country, all donations are just that; given for altruism, no money involved.

Someone had to be blamed. Perhaps the prostitutes hanging round the ports waiting for the ships to come in. Perhaps the sailors in the 1800s who used the prostitutes. Let me blame the monkeys in Cameroon who the scientists speculated had harboured the virus and started its worldwide spread.

Wherever it came from, Alexa would never forget her patients particularly the angel-faced Christopher and Timothy the ankle biter. Rest in peace.

But there was one more enigmatic tale to be told.

One evening as Alexa was getting ready to go home Bel, the head of the transfusion department came in. 'Cancel your plans for tonight; there is a very sick lady arriving from Africa. She is in late pregnancy, unconscious and we are requested to stay here to monitor her throughout the night. She is the wife of a missionary. Don't know which country she has come from, somewhere in Africa.'

Numerous other people were also donating their care and expertise to keep this lady alive. After an exhausting night, Alexa said to Bel, 'Well, she is still with us.'

Bel, a good lady with deep faith, replied, 'Of course; this lady and her child will survive.'

'You are a bit more optimistic than most. She is barely alive,' replied Alexa.

Bel explained, 'You see, the Mission House in Africa contacted the next house; they contacted the next one in line so eventually this lady was supported by a ring of prayer right round the world.'

'Hm,' muttered Alexa. 'This will need a bit more than divine intervention.'

Bel and Alexa collected their samples from what appeared to be a large mound attached to numerous drips and cylinders, in a very dimly lit room and carried out their tests throughout the night. Three days later when hope was diminishing, the patient, contrary to expectation, opened her eyes. Slowly, slowly, she recovered and after some weeks produced a healthy baby.

'Makes you think, doesn't it, Fluff? Makes you think.'

Her memories spent, she had no wish to return to any more. That was it. Career over.

With that, she and Fluff retired to the spare room to spend their last night on a rock-hard mattress and not very warm duvet.

Next morning Alexa said a tearful goodbye to Mrs Nicholls. With all the goods loaded into the furniture van, Fluff settled in her basket beside her, she set off for the long, now familiar journey, to start a new life.

'Come and visit me,' she called out to Mrs Nicholls as she tearfully waved goodbye.

'I would love to, but I don't know how. I will sort that one out. Bye.'

Chapter 20

Following the struggle to get the furniture van down to the cottage, the replacement of beds with millimetres to spare on the staircase and the remainder of her goods and chattels dumped on the living room floor she had, at last, a home to her liking. With her books in order, her painting materials stacked for quick access to the patio if the light was right, her favourite paintings on the walls. Yes, she could live here.

A visit to Falmouth reminded her of Roisin's fascination with the big ships that went to the world. 'What had happened to her?' she wondered. She resolved to contact Philip to see if he had any news.

Life in Cornwall was idyllic. A cottage with a magical view for painting or just to gaze at. A village shop with an owner who still greeted her with a miaow and called her cat lady. Then the delightful people she met up with at the local pub; the people who gave so much of their time and effort but had so little themselves. Perhaps she should invite them to lunch but perhaps that might seem a little patronising.

It was time to invite dear old Mrs Nicholls down for a holiday.

'Ullo. Who's that?' came a voice on the other end of the line.

'It's me, Alexa. I thought you might like to pay me a visit. Fluff and I have missed you.'

'I don't know how to get there.'

'I will sort it out for you. I'll get a train ticket for you from Slough to Truro. My friend John will pick you up and take you to Slough and put you on the train. I'll be waiting on the platform at Truro then we can drive out to the cottage. Let me know when you want to come.'

'I should love to come.'

'Good. Just let me know the date. OK? Bye for now.'

A week later, Mrs Nicholls rang. 'Alexa. Can I come a week on Friday? Will that give you enough time to arrange it?'

Tickets were bought and posted. John called Ms N.to make himself known and the following Friday was picked up, taken to Slough and put on the train.

'Look after 'er,' said John to the porter, holding out a ten-pound note, 'and put her out at Truro; someone will meet her there.'

'Right mate.' He slipped the note into his pocket. 'I'll deal with your case.' Mrs Nicholls was settled into a seat on the left side so she would get a good view where the track ran alongside the sea in Devon. She was nervous but so far so good; she even felt a little excited. After a long journey, when she had dozed off, she heard, 'Next station, Truro. Please take all your belongings.'

'Oh. I think this is where I have to get off.'

'Let me see your ticket,' said the man sitting opposite. 'Yes. This is it. Truro. Move up to the door and I will get your case. Which one? The bright red one. Very sensible.'

He jumped off the train, dragging the case down to the platform and helped Mrs Nicholls get down.

'Bye,' he called out. 'Enjoy your holiday,' and nimbly stepped up to get on board again.

'What a nice man. Now don't panic. Where is Alexa?'

'I'm here,' a voice called out as Alexa ran across the platform and hugged the old lady. 'Mrs N. How lovely to see you. Did you have a good journey?'

'Oh yes. The scenery was wonderful and people so kind.'

'Come on then,' said Alexa towing the wheelie case behind her. 'Let's get home. You must be dying for a cup of tea.'

Through Truro, on to Falmouth then down the lane to Porth Abbas. The hedgerows were still in bloom, Mrs N exclaiming at the colour. 'It is beautiful.'

'Not far now,' as they went down the lane and stopped outside the cottage.

Looking down the creek, the sun shining on the water, the view out to sea stunning but new to Mrs N; they both sat and looked.

'My dear,' said the old lady. 'I have never seen anything like it; it makes me want to cry.'

'Have a pasty before you do then you can look some more. Let's get your luggage indoors.'

As Alexa opened the door to the cottage, Fluff came running to Mrs N., miaowing and rubbing round her legs.

'She remembers me.' She picked her up and hugged her. 'Oh, my lovely puss.'

Alexa put the pasties in the oven to warm up and made a cup of tea.

'I suggest you have a rest after lunch. You have had a long and tiring journey.'

Pasties dealt with, Alexa led the old lady over to the settee, put a cushion behind her head, covered her with a duvet and within five minutes she was fast asleep. She awoke in the early evening and walked to the window to look out. The sun was going down and spreading a glow across the creek, the trees gradually disappearing as the light faded.

'I could just sit and watch this; it is so beautiful.'

'It will be there tomorrow,' said Alexa. 'Do you want the television on?'

'No dear. I want to chat with you and find out about your life here.'

They chattered away accompanied with cups of tea until Alexa noticed that Mrs N's head kept drooping.

'Let's go to bed; it has been a long day.' Together they went up the stairs.

There were more oohs and aahs about the prettily decorated room.

'You get into bed,' said Alexa, 'then I'll turn off your bedside lamp and see you in the morning. Fluff and I will bring you a cup of tea.' She looked in ten minutes later; Mrs N. was fast asleep.

Alexa accompanied by Fluff took up a cup of tea and was now sitting on Mrs N.'s bed discussing plans for the day. 'As it is such a lovely day,' said Alexa, 'I thought you might like to spend your first day here. We can explore later.'

The sat on the patio overlooking the creek, Alexa painting, Mrs N. just looking. At one point, she squealed, 'There's a boat with people on board.'

'Yes. They take people to look at the end of the creek, but they have to turn around pretty quickly because of the tide. There's a house there where the women of the village used to gut and clean pilchards; horrible job; their hands were red raw.'

So the days passed, one day at the cottage, the next out visiting the villages on the coast.

'It's all so beautiful. No wonder you want to live here.'

One day they went to the posh village shop. 'Good miaow to you, cat lady. I see you have brought a friend. Did you come by broomstick?' Rob laughed.

'No. We are parked outside. There was no room for two people on the broomstick. We'll have some of your home cured ham, please.'

'Certainly. Your friend can choose which type she wants.'

Delighted, Mrs N. chose honey with herbs.

'There's a sale at the pub on Saturday. Go along,' he said to Mrs N. 'You can make some new friends.'

'We shall go,' said Alexa. 'They sell the most gorgeous cream scones.'

'Why do they say miaow to you?' asked Mrs N.

'It's just a joke. Someone saw the cats following me around the fields and asked if they sat on my broomstick. They are nice people and I go along with it. It is all just a bit of fun.'

During the week, they visited some of the beauty spots; Porthleven, Cadgwith.

'We are going somewhere particularly special today.' As Alexa packed a picnic into a basket.

'Oh, where?'

'It's a surprise.'

Taking the ferry across the River Fal was a great excitement. Along the narrow lanes and turning off at the sign for St Just in Roseland. 'My favourite place in all of Cornwall,' said Alexa.

They parked the car and walked across to the lychgate. Beyond lay the most stunning view. A path lined with stones inscribed with poetry led down to an ancient church with square tower. The churchyard was amass with rhododendrons of every hue and the beds teemed with wildflowers.

The creek spread out beyond the church, a small boat with a red sail billowing in the wind. It called out for artists. *I must come back here to paint*, thought Alexa. 'It is said by H.V. Morton that this is the most beautifully situated church in the whole of the UK.'

'I think he got it right,' said Mrs N. 'It is my favourite now.'

'Do you want to look around the church?'

'I should love to.'

Inside all was peace and stillness. They stopped to look at the board of the clergy who had served here since the church was founded in AD550. Mrs N. said a silent prayer for all in the world and for having found such a beautiful place.

'Let's find a beach and have lunch. Porthluney with Caerhayes castle as the background fitted the bill. The castle is not terribly old, built on the site of a much older one but it is such a romantic setting.'

They enjoyed their picnic then set off for home.

St Just in Roseland Church, Cornwall

'What a wonderful day,' announced Mrs N. when they arrived back at the cottage. 'Thank you so much, Alexa. I never thought I would get to Cornwall.'

'You are very welcome. I love going back to visit these places and, of course, so much more enjoyable in your company. We'll have a quiet day tomorrow and then off to the pub sale on Saturday.'

With a painting tucked under her arm, off they went.

'Why are you taking a painting?'

'I always take one. They sell them for the Penzance Lifeboat Fund.'

'You are such a good artist...' she hesitated. 'Could you let me have one sometime then I can tell my friends about my lovely holiday?'

160

'Of course. What would you like? I am only an amateur dauber, you know, but I should love to paint you a picture.'

'St Just in Roseland Church, please. Such a beautiful building and the setting is amazing.' She started to cry.

'I hope those are tears of joy,' said Alexa.

'They certainly are,' as she wiped the tears away.

The pub sale was a success as usual and Mrs N. made a few more friends.

'Lovely to see you. Come again, won't you?' said Dorothy.

'What lovely ladies, all so friendly.'

After alternate days of sightseeing and resting at the cottage, the holiday was nearly over.

'I should get your packing done tonight so we can make an early start tomorrow,' advised Alexa. 'Would you like to live down here? Do you think this life would suit you? You know that you are welcome.'

'I want to go home and think about it. It might sound odd, but Cornwall is almost too beautiful. Do you understand?'

'I know what you mean. To bed. You have a long day ahead of you. I have arranged for John to meet you at Slough; you can't miss him, the tallest man on the platform.'

The following day, Mrs Nicholls having given Fluff a farewell hug, helped Alexa load the luggage including a bag containing pasties, Cornish cream and scones into the car.

The old lady took a last look down the creek, absorbing it into her memory.

'You'll be back,' said Alexa; 'it will still be here.'

Mrs N. threw her arms around Alexa. 'Thank you for everything.'

'I'll see you next year or sooner if you wish,' replied Alexa.

At the station, Alexa saw Mrs N into the right seat on the right train and waved her on her way.

A letter came for Alexa. *Cornwall is such a beautiful place. I might get used to it if I lived there full time. I should like to come down once a year. That way, I shall always have something to look forward to.*

'Fine,' thought Alexa. *The weather is not always as perfect as we had for your holiday. We can have long periods of wind, cold and rain. You might get lonely on the days I have to go out. What a wise old lady; a sensible decision.*

Mrs Nicholls spent many holidays in Cornwall. She eventually died there, peacefully, in her sleep. The local community turned out in force, singing her on her way at the funeral. 'To a better place,' as the minister said though there was no better place than Alexa's cottage with its view as Mrs N. had long determined.

Some months later, on a warm, sunny day, Alexa, accompanied by Fluff, took Mrs Nicholl's ashes and tipped them into the creek. She stood watching, as on an ebb tide, they floated down and out to the open sea.

Chapter 21

A phone call came from Philip Warren.

'Meet me in Falmouth for a cup of coffee,' he said. 'That place that overlooks the harbour.'

'Anything wrong?'

'Just a few things to catch up on. Next Wednesday OK? About eleven?'

'Yes. See you then.' She put the phone down. 'I hope there is nothing wrong. It is so many years ago since I met Philip to return Roisin to her family,' she mused.

Philip Warren looked well, a little overweight, but friendly as ever. He gave Alexa a kiss on both cheeks. They found a table and ordered coffee.

After enquiring about each other, Alexa said, 'What's the news?'

'Well, a nosy councillor is poking his snout in and trying to insist the Council should look into the rumour that a group is living on the moor.'

'Why can't they leave things alone? They are not doing anyone harm.'

'I thought we could take a walk up there sometime,' said Philip, 'and see how they are.'

'We might not be welcome.'

'I think it will be OK if we tell them who we are. Roisin should recognise us.' They agreed to meet in a week's time, drive out to the layby on the A30 and try to find the path which led them to the spot where Roisin had disappeared.

On a windy, damp morning, walking sticks in hand, Philip and Alexa struggled up the hill and found the path, somewhat overgrown, which bordered the moor. As the path veered sharply to the left and uphill Philip said, 'I think this is it.' He pushed and pulled at the bushes which eventually gave way and he found himself in a glen shaded by very tall trees. In the distance, he heard the gurgling of a stream.

Going back to the bushes, he pushed his way back to Alexa. 'I think this is it. I can hear the river. Come on through. Mind how you go; it is very prickly.'

Alexa carefully negotiated her way. 'I feel sure this is the place. Shall we go on?'

Cautiously they went down through the glen following the sounds of the river. As they started up the slope, a man appeared. He was dressed in brown trousers and jacket and stood staring at the intruders.

'May we talk to you, please?' said Philip. 'We mean you no harm.'

The man came a little nearer. 'Who are you? What do you want?' He looked more nervous than angry.

'We are Alexa and Philip. Many years ago, we brought Roisin back here. She suddenly disappeared and we should like to know if she is safe.'

'I am forever grateful to you. She is my daughter,' the man replied. 'Yes, she is well. Would you like to come and meet her?'

'We would love to meet her,' piped up Alexa. 'It is kind of you to invite us.'

'Right. Follow me.'

They walked along the riverbank, then up a slope and found themselves facing a small paddock housing a couple of horses and a cow. There was a barn containing bales of hay. Chickens clucked and scrabbled in an area clearly built just for them.

They walked on past an area given over to growing vegetables and corn.

'Come,' he said. 'You can meet Roisin. I'll send someone to fetch her.'

Down in the combe Alexa and Philip gazed in amazement at the houses built by the group. 'Come in and meet Grace; she has looked after Roisin since she was a baby. Her mother died young. In fact, Grace looks after us all.'

Young James came panting in followed by a beautiful young woman.

'Are you ill, Father?'

'No-no. I have a surprise for you.' He turned to introduce their visitors.

Roisin stared for a moment in confusion then Alexa stepped forward. 'We are Alexa and Philip. You stayed with me for a short while and then we brought you home or at least we hoped you had got back safely.'

Roisin flew into Alexa's arms crying, 'I am so pleased to see you.'

'Will you eat with us?' asked James senior. 'Our fare is simple but you are very welcome.'

Grace laid out platters plus two for the visitors and placed on each a large piece of homemade bread and a chunk of cheese as the members of the group assembled for the mid-day meal. As Grace made tea, James introduced Alexa and Philip.

'I say this from all of us,' said Fred. 'You are most welcome. We are so grateful that Roisin was returned to us.'

They all tucked into their lunch and all except James senior went back to their work.

'We need to talk, James,' said Philip.

'I will go over to see Stella for a while,' said Grace sensing there were things that needed to be discussed.

'Will you sit down?' said James. 'I imagine it is something important you have to say.'

'I am afraid so. A mischievous member of the Council has reported that you and your group are living on the moor. The vast majority of the people are quite happy with the arrangement; you are self-sufficient, you make no trouble. In fact, many did not even know you are here. Now that the fact has been reported the Council are bound to look into it.'

'You see, legally you are committing an offence simply by being on the moor which contravenes the rules of the National Park regulations and secondly, you do not pay tax which some people resent. I am sorry to be the bringer of bad news.'

James, clearly an intelligent man, faced Philip. 'What will happen to us?'

'I don't know. If they make you move, they create a problem for themselves as they don't want you wandering the lanes always trying to find somewhere to stay.'

'What do you suggest?' asked James.

'Just stay put. Carry on as you usually do. Alexa and I will talk to the Council. Madam Chairman is a reasonable and sensitive lady. Any proposal will take years to get through Council legislation, so you are safe for the time being. We will keep in touch with you. Thank you for allowing us to visit and talk with you. We both admire what you have accomplished here.'

They all stood up and shook hands.

'I will see you back to where you came in. It will be easier for you to enter by the lane near the old quarry next time. Come through the village and look for a gap wide enough to get a horse and cart through, then follow the road to the old quarry.'

James turned and strode away. Alexa and Philip followed the river, walked through the glen and found the path that led round the blackthorn hedge and eventually down to the layby and the car.

James went back to work. He had sheltered and looked after the group for around ten years. Always in the back of his mind he knew this day would come. Now came the big decision. Should he tell his "family" or should he shield them for as long as possible? All afternoon as he worked on the vegetable patch, he debated the matter in his head. As the light faded and they all wended their way to James's house to get cleaned up for the evening meal he had made his decision. *I shall not tell them until it is necessary. There is no point in upsetting them.* That evening as he said the prayer thanking God for their good fortune, James silently added, 'Please look after my people.' Then they all sat down and chattered, sharing the day's news as Grace dished out the excellent stew.

When the others had dispersed to their separate homes and the tidying up completed, Grace said to James, 'It was nice of Alexa and Philip to visit us. What did they really come for?' She was a shrewd old soul and had picked up on James's mood.

'Nothing for you to worry about. They had heard a rumour and wanted the chance to check on Roisin. I was pleased to see them. They are our friends. Bed now. We all have an early start.'

They all climbed into their bunks, James to worry the night away.

Chapter 22

Alexa and Philip reached the car in sober mood. Still not speaking, Philip drove back to Falmouth. They were both stunned by the consequences of their visit and the battles to come.

'I shall start looking into the legal side of things and see what can be done,' said Alexa. 'Let us keep in touch. Bye Philip.' She touched his cheek in farewell.

After a few days, Alexa got her act together and started consulting the Internet and made a visit to Falmouth library to gain any information she could. It was rather depressing; it would seem as if the Council and the Dartmoor National Park had right on their side.

At the Council office, Madam Chairman scanned the agenda for next month's meeting. 'What's this?' she enquired of the secretary. 'People living on the moor? That's not our problem. Refer it to the National Park committee.'

'Well, apparently it is as they have not been paying Council tax for many years.'

'Who has brought this forward? Hang on. I think I know; it is Dan something. When Councillor Yeo died, he felt it his duty to pursue the problem. Put it to the end of the list,' she said to the girl. 'I am sure there won't be time enough to discuss it. They can't have given us any trouble or the Council would have heard about it before now. Anything else?'

'No Madam. I will get that typed and circulated.'

'Thank you.' She went down the corridor, let herself in and sat down behind her desk. 'Now who can I ask about this?' She sat for a while then, 'I suppose the Dartmoor National Park committee is the most logical place to start.' She picked up the phone. 'Can you get the Chairman at Dartmoor National Park to phone me?' she said to the secretary. 'I don't have the number. Not urgent.'

'That should get them off my back for a while. As if I don't have enough to do. I am more concerned about getting planning permission for those starter homes we want to build off the motorway.'

Alexa, used to scanning documents, quickly went through the Council minutes for the last ten years. A small number of housing projects had been granted but none, it would seem on Dartmoor. Next, she went through the rules of the moor. A few buildings, mostly farms, had been allowed extensions or small barns in which to house cattle or store hay. There was no mention of a site where a small group had been granted land or permission to build, or even occupy land. Going through what documents she could find, restrictions on the moor were strict. For example, you could only pitch a tent for a maximum of two days. Alas, the group's presence on the moor was illegal.

Alexa, fortified by constant large mugs of tea, and distracted by Fluff's habit of walking across the computer keyboard, was beginning to think there was no way around the problem. James's group would be turned off the moor, the place where they had quietly lived for so many years.

The one advantage was that if the Council and the Dartmoor authorities turned them off—Where would they go? Alexa ruefully admitted that if she were not linked with the travellers' group, she would be shouting as loudly as the rest to remove these undesirables. But she had had to make a choice and in this instance there was no question which side she was batting for. She would go on searching, there had to be answer.

What happened in other counties around the UK? She decided to go through the minutes of each Council meeting to see if she could get a clue. It was a huge task so Alexa systematically worked her way through the documents. Most of them shifted the problem sideways with the problem being deferred from meeting to meeting and travellers parking on verges and leaving their mess behind for the local authority to clear up.

There is quite a number of sites situated around England. The north seems to be more sensitive than the south, perhaps they have the largest number of families to deal with, Liverpool being the main port from Ireland.

But who are all these people who want to come to England? The Irish travellers, distinct from the gypsies, with their distinctive way of life, have been an indigenous group in Ireland since ancient times. Where they originally came from seem obscure. In more recent times, general poverty and the Potato Famine drove many families to try for a better life elsewhere.

Alexa gave up her national search and concentrated on looking for small parcels of land in the Devon area where owners might be willing to sell.

Alexa fixed an appointment with Madam Chairman at the Council.

'We can afford to be a little less formal. I am Marion Drake, call me Marion.'

'Alexa. Philip Warren, a retired policeman, is working with me.'

'I know Philip. Good man. How come you are involved in this?'

'I met them years ago. They are good people trying to live a quiet life. I didn't know they planned to live on the moor. They are not doing any harm.'

'I wish I could help you,' said Marion. 'It would certainly solve a problem for the Council.'

Even if a piece of land was found, there were an enormous number of legalities to go through. The solicitors would be very busy for years to come.

Alexa turned to Marion. 'I know they have not been paying taxes and allowing them to stay is setting a precedent. Vans would be coming from all over England trying to reserve a patch. The Dartmoor National Park has to be protected. I appreciate all this. I will still keep trying. Thank you for your time, Marion. I know you are a busy lady.'

While sitting in the Council office, another line of enquiry had struck her. What about private land or land belonging to companies and firms? She set off home quite pleased that she had something else to look into. She was not giving up yet.

Back at the cottage, Alexa dragged out a chair on to the patio, made the inevitable cup of tea and sat contemplating the magnificent view and the endless problem of the travellers. The view always calmed her; she did not feel any sense of tranquillity regarding the travellers, only trouble ahead.

She was tired. *I shall take two weeks off, visit my friends at the pub, do a bit of painting then start again,* she thought.

It was a nice day, dancing sunlight and a light breeze. 'Come on Fluff. Let's go for a walk,' so off they went, down the garden, along the shore and back up the lane. 'This is what it is meant to be,' she said to Fluff. 'We must learn to relax.'

Alexa refused to think about her new plan and spent many happy days painting followed by a visit to the pub for lunch and a chat with the ladies of the village. On one occasion, she met Tom Banham and they chatted and laughed for an hour. Such nice people.

Alexa put away her "toys" and began to concentrate once more on the travellers. It was the talk of private land that had given her a new direction. The Council had investigated every available inch of space in their area with no result. 'The one possibility,' thought Alexa, 'is to try the commercial companies.

If they had a bit of land unsuitable for their purposes, they might well be glad of a bit of rent or income.' It was worth a try.

She phoned Philip keep him in the loop and promised to ask for his help if anything came of the enquiries.

She went online to list the business and building companies in Devon and north Cornwall.

Next she composed a letter asking if their company had a small, maybe three or four acres, piece of unused or unsuitable for their purpose, land which could be given over and, with help from the Council, house five caravans or dwellings to a group of people who now have to leave their current site. They are a good, quiet, self-sufficient collection of folk who had lived in the same place for the last ten years with no problems and now need a new home.

With forty letters printed and put into envelopes, she now had only to address them, stick on the stamps and get them sent off. It was becoming a time-consuming and expensive venture, particularly the postage which had increased so much recently. Any hope of an answer meant including a stamped addressed envelope. Add on a pack of A4 paper and a couple of ink cartridges and she would soon be out with her begging bowl. But if she got any sort of response, it would have been worth it.

At the posh shop in the village which also served as a post office, she was greeted with, 'Good miaow to you. Did you come by cat?'

'No. I left her at home. Only one left now. Could you stick these letters in your collection bag? It will save me a bit of work shoving them all in the post box.'

'Of course. You giving a party?' as he dumped the pile of letters in the bag.

'No, but I might if this lot pays off. You will be included on the guest list. Thanks.'

There being no likelihood of a reply for at least a couple of weeks, Alexa returned to the life she had intended for herself, walking, painting and relaxing.

Several weeks later, Alexa came in to find a couple of envelopes on the mat.

Recognising them as her "return" letters, she quickly tore them open to find, as expected, that they unable to help but wished the moor group well. 'Oh well. No surprise there,' she muttered. 'Early days yet.'

Some never replied but one day she opened up a grubby-looking reply, 'I might be able to help you. Come and see me.'

The letter was headed Michael Lennon Builders. Local, an Irish name. Could there be some hope here?

Alexa promptly got on the phone to Philip who said he would find out what he could but certainly would accompany Alexa to meet a possible helper.

Michael Lennon was a brash, hardworking man who had worked his way up, taking on any job available, mostly those other people did not want. He had a loyal pack of fellow countrymen who were grateful for a wage and somewhere to live. A row of dwellings built by the men themselves now existed behind a screen of trees. They were legal, just. The Council was willing to turn a blind eye to small problems if it got a few more off the housing list.

Michael, in the local pub, having heard of the plight of the group on the moor, said to his foreman one morning, 'Donald. Come and have a cup of coffee with me tomorrow and bring the site plans with you.'

'Right boss.' *What was he up to now?* Michael would help a fellow in distress if he could so long as it was also to the benefit of Michael Lennon, Builders.

Donald came into the office with a large wad of paper under his arm and put it down.

'Susie, bring us some coffee, love.' Which she promptly did and left.

'Have a cup,' said Michael. 'Whisky makes it taste better.' Opening the drawer of his desk and bringing out a large bottle of Scotch. 'No Irish, I'm afraid,' and poured a substantial dose into Donald's coffee. 'Right then. What do you know about an Irish group living up on Dartmoor?'

'Not a lot,' replied Donald. 'A few rumours. They don't cause any trouble, or we would have heard about them.'

Looking at the site map of his property, Michael said, 'Will you take me up to this bit of wasteland we have up here?'

'Sure. The jeep's outside.'

Michael Lennon had done well for himself. He now owned many acres of Devon with a large, once stately home hidden from the road by a clump of trees. With his itinerant workforce always seeking labour, he had been able to bring the building up to liveable standard for limited outlay. He treated the lads in a strict but kindly manner, so they were always willing to work for him.

It was more of a modern day fiefdom than lord of the manor, but the system worked.

Donald drove the boss up to a parcel of land sectioned off by a fence and again hidden from the road by a belt of trees. A rough and muddy track led off to the main road beyond; another in slightly better condition led up from the big house.

They got out of the jeep. 'Bloody Hell,' shouted Michael. 'What do we have here?' looking aghast at huge piles of brickwork, old iron and any sort of rubbish you could think about.

'It's all the old rubbish from the building sites. You told us to put it here so you don't have to pay the Council fees at the tip.'

'So I did, Donald, so I did. I slipped up there.'

'What are you planning, boss?'

'Find out about the group on the moor and report back to me. I have a plan, Donald.'

'Sure,' replied Donald, knowing when to keep quiet. 'Enough? I'll take you back to the house.'

'Don't worry, lad. You'll still have a job and a home.'

Half a dozen small concrete buildings were scattered around the grounds masquerading as sheds or barns but providing homes for the main workforce.

Donald was happy to live in one of these; no one asked questions about minor details like planning permission.

Donald had on occasions met Philip Warren when he was still on the force but he remained a useful contact. 'Let's go for a pint,' suggested Donald so once settled in the bar of the pub overlooking the harbour, Philip looked Donald in the eye and demanded, 'What does Michael want to know?'

'No beating about the bush with you. What do you know about a group living on the moor?'

'Why does Michael want to know?'

'He might have a bit of land he could offer the Council; if there is something in it for Michael.'

'Go on,' said Philip.

'If Michael could come to some arrangement, he might get the Council out of a hole and make a bit for himself.'

'What land are we talking about?'

'A plot of about five acres hidden from the road by trees. We were up there a couple of weeks ago; it is in a terrible state but Michael says if the Council wants it badly enough, they'll pay to have the rubbish removed. Run in some gas, water and electricity and it would solve the problem.'

'Not quite that simple. but perhaps we could set up a meeting between Michael and James, the leader of the group, to negotiate. There's a lady I should like to bring along. She has a sharp mind and cares about the travellers so she would be a useful ally. Long story; tell you sometime. See what you can do, Donald, and keep me posted. I have to go now but we will keep in touch.'

'Look,' said Donald, 'Michael Lennon is a rough, tough man but there is a heart in there somewhere and I feel he will help his countrymen if he can—even if they come from the north,' he said dryly.

'Bye now.' They shook hands and went on their way.

Philip promptly phoned Alexa who suggested that he come over to the cottage and they talk about it. 'I'm quite a good cook so come for lunch.'

A week later, Philip and Alexa sat on the patio overlooking the fabulous view down the creek to where it opened out to the sea.

'Some place you have got yourself here. How come?' asked Philip.

'I had a lovely old great-aunt who had nobody else to leave it to, so she left it to me.'

'I have the feeling you were a bit kind to your dear old aunt,' said Philip.

'Well. I tried to be. I had no idea she owned a cottage in Cornwall and even less that she would leave it to me. I used to take her for a drive in the country and then on for a cream tea at a local hotel. She really enjoyed it. Lovely old lady. The cottage was rather rundown but when I sold my flat near London, I was able to modernise it and make it a home. I never cease to be grateful to Great Aunt Alice.' She turned to Philip. 'Lunch first then we can get down to business.'

'Sounds good to me.' They ambled through the kitchen with its delicious smells and on into the living room. 'My goodness. You can cook as well,' said Philip later. 'No end to your talents,' after putting away venison pie and Cornish cream trifle.

'No dozing allowed. I'll bring the coffee out to the patio.'

Once settled, Philip asked, 'Do you know about Michael Lennon?'

'No. Who is he?'

'You must have seen them. Lennon Builders.'

'I have seen them. I don't know the company.'

'Michael, better known as Irish Mick. That is what we used to call him. He will do anything to make money. I have to hand it to him he has worked hard, joining in the labouring himself if needs be. So, when this plot of land with stately home in a state of collapse came up for sale, Michael stuck his oar in and purchased it.'

'Tell me more.'

'A very old gentleman, the last in a long line, didn't leave a will. The remaining relatives just wanted rid of the place, just wanted the money so when Irish Mick heard about it he put his solicitor onto it and bought the lot for a reasonable amount. There was little competition for it. The land was in a terrible state and there was no building permission, not that that worried Mick. He would find a way round it somehow. His lawyer was one of those clever dicks who knew just about every trick in the book. You know, like the chap in London who all the rich business men hire to get them off their motoring offences.'

'I am beginning to get the picture,' said Alexa. 'Everything just within the law.'

'Anyhow,' continued Philip, 'Mick got his stately home rebuilt in a somewhat vulgar style with highly coloured gardens all round, but he was happy with it. His boys had worked hard on the building and were well rewarded.'

'I don't quite see what this has to do with James's group on the moor,' intervened Alexa.

'Hang about; that's coming. Mick heard about the problem one night in the pub. and having a piece of rubbish-strewn land not being used smelt a deal. He would also gain kudos in the Irish community if he managed to find these folks a place to live.'

'Why don't you and I,' said Alexa, 'go up and talk to James and arrange a meeting with Mick and his lawyer? I will do anything to help them but it must be legal.'

'Absolutely,' said Philip. 'Now can I finish my coffee and take in some more of this wonderful view! What is the little river right opposite?' he asked.

'That's Frenchman's Creek of du Maurier fame.'

'Have a bit of trouble getting your ship up there.'

'I know but it makes for a good tale.'

They said goodbye after a couple more hours with at least an idea in their heads, if not a solution.

'Will you come again?' asked Alexa.

'I should love to.'

'Good. Let us meet up with James and see what he thinks, and take it from there.'

Chapter 23

Some weeks later, Philip drove Alexa around the village at the foot of the moor and found the lane leading to James's encampment. It was certainly an easier way in without the exhausting climb up from the motorway.

Having parked the car, they climbed down into the combe where the main houses were built and looked around for James. They once more admired these cunningly built dwellings of branches, clay and straw and hidden under the tall pines growing overhead.

Grace was the first to spot them and jumped back in alarm, running into the nearest house.

'Grace,' called out Alexa. 'Don't be frightened; it is Alexa and Philip come to see James.'

The old lady's white and frightened face came peered round the door. 'Shall I be making you a cup of tea while I send someone to find James? You boy,' she called out to the young man stacking hay. 'James. Find your dad and tell him he has visitors, nice ones.'

'Yes Grace,' and ran off down the field.

A few minutes later, James senior came in. Tall and dignified, he extended his hand to Philip. 'It is good to see you. I trust you have news.'

The strain was obviously telling on James, he looked thinner and his face pale despite his outdoor living.

'Well, a few encouraging signs. You have met Alexa, haven't you?'

'Do you want me to go, James?' asked Grace. 'I can go over to Stella's.'

'No, my dear. You know a deal about our situation. You stay but don't talk to the others.'

They all sat down with cups of tea and Philip and Alexa tried to explain the situation with Michael Leeson and the Council.

'He has invited you to meet him and discuss the problem. I think you should take up his offer,' said Philip.

'Thank you. I will do anything you suggest. I know you are trying to help us.'

'Michael always cunningly operates just within the law, and he has a solicitor who is twice as clever as he is. Right. I will arrange a meeting and let you know. I'll pick you up by car. Alexa will be there to add her ideas and support.'

They all stood up and shook hands. 'Thank you for the tea, Grace,' added Alexa. And with that they made their departure.

A few weeks later, with James next to Philip and Alexa in the back seat, they approached Michael's estate. Parking in front of the superb and original ironwork gates, a voice called out, 'Who are you?'

Philip shut down the engine and shouted out of the window. 'Philip Warren with James Kelly and Alexa Moray to meet Michael Leeson.'

'You can come in. Follow the road.' The gates slowly opened.

Philip followed the well-kept driveway and fetched up outside an elaborate, carved door nestling under a stone portico. A young girl was waiting for them and called, 'Good morning. Mr Lennon is expecting you.'

'We met previously. I am Philip Warren. You must be Susie.'

'Indeed. Please come in.'

They entered into a large hallway decorated with numerous paintings, an eclectic collection. With a hurried glance around, Alexa thought, *I should like to study some of these. Michael either has good taste or too much money.*

Susie led the visitors into a very large, high-ceilinged room stuffed with furniture. Her father, being a cabinet maker and pieces of furniture coming in for repair all the time, Alexa immediately recognised a Chippendale cabinet and then a piece of Gillow. Putting her hand down for support she encountered a knobbly piece and on closer inspection saw that it was a carved mouse, the trademark of Robert Houseman. She smiled in pleasure.

'You like my wee mousie?' called out Michael.

'Indeed, I do. I have one on an ashtray but yours is much better example.'

'Come on then. Let's get started. Susie. Where's that coffee?'

'Coming, Michael.' She pushed in a trolley and started to fill the cups.

'Right. I am Michael. This is Donald, my estate manager, and this is Nick, my lawyer,' as he pointed out a handsome young man in an expensive suit and shiny black ankle boots; he oozed confidence.

Opposing were Philip, Alexa and all important one, James Kelly who looked pale and nervous.

'What is it that you are wanting, James, from me?' demanded Michael. James looked tense and nervous at being addressed so directly.

'A small group including myself need a place to live. The Dartmoor National Park and the local Council have decided they cannot allow us to live on the moor any longer.'

'Why, suddenly after all this time?'

'Someone complained and legally we have no right to be there, so we have to go. But where? that is the problem. Councils in England have a statutory duty to house us or provide land but there is little available, and we are not wanted anyway.'

'How many are there in your group?' asked Michael.

'Twelve. We have a small area for growing crops. We have to buy in animal feed, mostly from farmers markets, and this is stored in barrels and metal containers. At present, we have a small, grassed area where we keep a pony, an older horse, an old cow to provide milk. And a dozen chickens. There are three travellers' vans, one of which is being lived in by a young woman and her son.

'Where is your water supply?' asked Nick.

'We take water from the stream below; it runs down from the moor so is quite pure.'

'And lastly, heating. What facilities do you have for washing and heating?'

'We heat the stoves with sawn up fallen branches. We do not damage any new trees. There are three wattle and daub cottages in the combe which we built ourselves and are hidden from view.'

Michael turned to Nick. 'Do you reckon we can help these people and,' he paused, 'get something out of it for us?'

'Difficult,' said Nick. 'But we can try. Down to details then. We (Michael) wants a short hardcore road leading into an area on which will be built five cottages. At present, there is an enormous amount of rubbish which will have to be cleared.'

'The Council can do that,' growled Michael.

'Alongside,' continued Nick, 'there will be allotment areas for growing crops, a grassed area on which to keep a few farm animals. The area will be hidden by a small belt of trees. The roadway will be difficult as it is on private land and the Council will be reluctant to pay. Gas, water and electricity will need to be laid on. The rest should not be too much of a problem. We need planning permission for the houses and over wintering for the animals. Remember that if the group is turned off the moor the Council has a statutory duty to provide them somewhere else to live. So, we have the upper hand.'

'Well,' intervened Philip, 'sounds a splendid idea but who will be paying for all this?'

'I will,' chipped in Michael.

'And what do you get out of this? I don't quite understand.'

'I'll put up the money for the cottages, the tenants pay rent to me. The Council will have taxes paid direct to them. Any insurances are the responsibility of the tenants.'

'You're a clever old sod. Sorry Alexa,' replied Philip.

'Worry not,' she replied. 'I have heard worse.'

'How do you think I got where I am?' retorted Michael. 'A cunning mind and a lot of expertise from Nick. Draw up a plan, Nick,' continued Michael. 'And you can show me the thirty-ninth draft (or however many it takes) and we will pay a visit to the Council solicitor and point out the error of his ways. And go from there. More coffee, anyone?'

Philip started to laugh, James looked petrified. Was this the way things were conducted on the outside?

Nick turned to James with a kindly smile. 'This will take a long time,' he said. 'But we will find your people a home. Carry on living as you were and I will keep you posted through Alexa and Philip.' For a moment, the arrogant look was knocked off his face. He turned to Alexa and Philip. 'Thank you for caring. We will find them a home.'

Michael was suddenly gone. Shouting back through the open door they heard, 'I have to go over to Okehampton to look at some roadworks. I'll drive myself. Take James to see the plot.'

'Yes Boss,' said Donald.

They all climbed into the Land Rover and Donald drove them behind the belt of trees screening the big house and stopped by the rubbish strewn plot.

'Don't look so appalled, James. Just examine if the size is adequate; it can all be cleared up in time.'

James looked at his possible future home in horror. Comparing it to the moor, his heart sank. Putting on his practical hat, he walked around the allotted area and realised that, yes there would be sufficient space for their needs, room for the vans, room to grow crops, a place for the horses and the cow, six new houses with water, gas and electricity and main drainage laid on. He suddenly felt thankful. This could happen.

'I will keep you informed,' said Donald. 'Let's go home.'

Donald took them back to Philip's car who returned James to his hideaway on the moor.

Turning to Alexa, Philip said, 'How did we get involved in this?'

Alexa paused. 'Some things you have to do, or I do and I have the feeling you are of the same mind, Philip.'

Life went on as usual up on the moor. James said nothing about the possible new plan. Why upset them before you need to?

Nick worked on the plan he had been set, producing draft after draft until Michael was satisfied. He then fixed an appointment with Robert the Council solicitor and the battle began.

'You don't want much, do you, Nick?'

'I only want a solution to this problem, and one has to be found.'

'With what Michael Lennon wants and a good cut for you.'

'That too.'

'Well, let me go through it before I approach Madam Chairman. She will want to be very sure of her ground before putting it to a Council meeting. So far, she has avoided the subject by putting it last on the agenda and then running out of time.'

At long last, the two solicitors agreed on a version that satisfied Michael and was fit to present to Madam Chairman.

Marion, an astute woman but kindly at heart, read the document many times, queried numerous points then said to Robert, 'This could work if we can get over the resentment of the local community about giving anything to a group of travellers though the alternative is of leaving them to roam the lanes to be abused just for living. Don't forget that we have a statutory duty to provide somewhere, permanent or transient, for these people to live.'

When Alexa got home and with tea and cat installed, she thought about the day's happenings. Surely James and his group had a right to life, as much as the rest of the population, but what did it actually mean? So once more it was back to the books and computer.

The law states that everyone shall be protected as laid down in the Protection of Human Rights Act, 1998. No one shall be deprived of his life save in the execution of a court sentence following a massive crime such as massacre, genocide or starvation of a whole population.

'Enough,' she said out loud. 'James is the total antithesis to this, caring and providing for his people over many years. He and his group have as much right to life as you or me.'

In the local pub, the talk was all of the coming Council meeting.

'One of us will have to go, after all the fuss old Yeo (God rest his soul) made,' said Dan. 'I'm going along to see the fun. If the travellers win this, you have done them a favour,' he paused and with a chuckle, 'and I don't think that is quite what Yeo intended.'

'Dirty lot. Why didn't they go somewhere else? We never wanted them here,' said another member of the group.

'Well. I don't like the ones who leave their muck and rubbish everywhere, but this lot have never caused any trouble. Should be a lively night.'

News spread about the Council meeting and for once there would be a good-sized audience in contrast to the few old faithfuls who generally turned up for a moan and free tea and biscuits.

Alexa would take advantage of the two minutes allowed to state the case on behalf of the travellers. Used to reading papers at scientific meetings, this held no fears for her but she went over and over her short speech consulting with Philip and Nick until she was satisfied.

Marion, Madam Chairman read and reread the document finally agreed by the two lawyers. The topic moved up the agenda and a Council meeting scheduled.

The villagers were highly interested, primarily to see what these people from the moor looked like, expecting men with uncut hair and dressed in sheepskins.

Instead they got well-dressed men in tweed jackets and corduroy trousers, hair and beards neatly trimmed. The audience was a bit disappointed.

A huge crowd was expected, and chairs were laid out in the largest of the Council chambers.

On the evening of the meeting with a jampacked hall, visitors flowing out into the corridor. Madam Chairman walked into the chamber followed by members of the Council and took their seats. Next came Alexa, Philip and Nick. Finally, the three representatives of the group on the moor came in. James, alongside Fred and Hugh walked to the three allotted chairs and sat down.

Small matters dealt with Madam Chairman introduced the possibility that the Council could assist in providing a new home for the travellers.

After outlining the part that the Council would have to commit to financially, she added, 'In no way do I condone the fact that the travellers have lived on the moor illegally and have paid no rent or taxes. But I do respect that James Kelly provided a home for his fellow travellers, caused no damage to the moor; in fact, may have contributed to its welfare. Michael Lennon has offered a piece of land on his estate to remain in his possession on which the travellers could live providing that the Council allow the building of five small cottages at his expense, and he would retain ownership of these. He would, as the law states, also expect that all other facilities be provided by the Council.'

Alexa was then asked to provide her short speech. She stood up, well-dressed, confident and spoke up, 'Madam Chairman and Council members. By an odd quirk of circumstance, I have got to know and understand a little of the life that most travellers are forced to live, shunted from pillar to post, shouted at, abused. James Kelly has done his best for his group, although like Madam Chairman I cannot condone the avoidance of rent or taxes but as we all have a legal right to life, then surely, we, as a community, should allow these people have one, too. They have caused no trouble; they have taken care of the part of the moor on which they lived. I ask you, waving her arm across the audience and the Council members, to allow these people to have a legal, permanent home.' As she sat down, she became aware of a burst of applause from the audience.

Councillor Dan, determined to put his oar in, shouted out, 'What about all the back tax. We had to pay. Why not them?'

The discussion went back quietly to the councillors. Madam Chairman stood up. 'I feel that we have progressed well this evening. There are many problems ahead, points to be discussed. I feel that we are closer to a solution. We shall convene here in one month's time to give a final verdict.'

Councillor Dan sat with face like a lemon.

'You can't win 'em all,' said Joe, another councillor, 'you've had your fun, Dan, now give it a rest.'

'I did it for Yeo,' said Dan.

'No, you didn't,' replied Joe. 'You just wanted to stir up a bit of trouble.'

All stood while Madam Chairman and the Councillors left the chamber. Some of the audience left for home; others stayed on to talk among themselves. Various comments floated up.

'I don't object to that providing the back taxes are paid. They aren't doing any harm and it keeps them off the roads.'

'Why should they get houses built for them when there's a queue of people for Council houses?'

'Well, if you had listened, you would have heard that Michael Lennon is footing the bill and will claim the rents.'

'Cunning old sod; he has got some scheme planned. Mick doesn't do anything unless there is something in it for him.'

'Well. I reckon he wants to keep the land but not the upkeep. He will get the area tidied up but still maintain ownership.'

'Yeah. You could be right.'

Eventually, the visitors were persuaded to go home and the warden thankfully switched off the lights and locked up.

Philip, in the car on the way back to the moor, said, 'James. You did well. I think you will win in the end. You have to be patient. These things take time. With a lot more discussion between the solicitors, we might even get a verdict at the next meeting in a month's time; unlikely still.' His voice tailed off.

James, Fred and Hugh squashed in the back of the car muttered among themselves. Finally, James spoke up, 'I cannot thank you and Alexa enough for all you are doing for us.'

'You are welcome. Do we get a cup of tea at your place?'

'Yes. Two if you wish.'

The optimistic view that a decision might be reached by the next meeting was delayed by an open letter delaying the decision for legal reasons.

Philip assured James that this was good news; the longer the Council took, the longer the group could stay on the moor. Madam Chairman was, of course, totally optimistic about the time it would take, primarily due to the obstruction of Councillor Dan. Eventually the document was considered fit to put to the vote, Councillor Dan having ungracefully given in.

Many months later, a further open meeting was held. The crowd was not so large this time, the decision to allow the travellers to live out of sight and at no extra cost to the rate payers seemed a reasonable outcome.

James, Fred and Hugh sat bemused as the Council voted in favour and the motion was passed.

'We have won,' said Philip. 'I know it will mean starting all over again but you now have a permanent home.'

The three men stood up and bowed to the Council members. 'Madam Chairman,' said James, 'we are grateful to you for the understanding of our position.' The poor man was nearly in tears. 'We, the group on the moor, thank you from the bottom of our hearts.'

The members filed out, feeling pleased with themselves, aware that a problem had been solved for the travellers and had got the Council out of a legal hole without too much expense involved, thanks to the cunning of Michael Lennon.

'Come on,' said Philip. 'I'll buy us all a drink to celebrate then you can go home, James, and tell your people they have a permanent home, albeit after a massive amount of work to get started again.'

After a drink at the local pub, they made their way to the site on the moor via the hole in the hedge, parked and walked on to the houses in the combe. Darkness was descending as everyone made their way to James's house for the evening meal.

'Before we eat, I have something to say,' said James.

They all looked to him in anxiety. He smiled. 'It is good news. For some time now, our home here on the moor has been in danger and we were faced with being turned back on to the lanes and roads and all the problems that brings. I am not proud of the fact that we have been living here illegally and after many years someone reported us.'

'For the last three years or so, Philip and Alexa have been trying to find us a permanent home, a place where we no longer have to live in fear of being found. I did not tell you what was going on; there was no point in upsetting you all.'

'Fred, Hugh and myself have attended the last three meetings at the Council where the new area was approved of as our new home. I will tell you all the details later. For now, we should thank Philip and Alexa for the enormous amount of work they put in on our behalf. We must now bow our heads in prayer and thank God for his guidance.'

Everyone stood up and put their hands together. James conducted a short service and amen was said by everyone.

'And now Grace, perhaps you would please dish up the supper.'

Grace, with tears in her eyes, hugged James. 'You are a good man. I have always thought of you as a son. I am proud to be your mother. And now we shall eat.'

With supper over, James explained where their new home would be. Roisin started to cry. 'But we are happy here. Why do we have to move?'

'We have no choice, but many things will be the same. We will still grow our own vegetables and keep the two horses, the cow and the chickens. Houses with hot and cold running water, gas and electricity will be provided. Just think. No more going down to the river on a freezing cold day.'

'When will this happen?' queried Stella.

'It will probably take eighteen months to a year. There is a road to be built and large amounts of rubbish taken away.'

'And how do we pay for all this?' asked Stella.

'It has all been worked out. Basically, we pay rent to Michael for the houses and Council tax to the Council. We shall go on as before, earning our keep. Michael will employ us men on any building or road works and we can continue to work on the farms during harvest time etc. We shall be self-sufficient, the women will continue to grow our fruit and vegetables.'

The Dartmoor National Park committee, after much debate, decided not to sue or press the group for back rent. James and his people had looked after the area, and it would in a short space of time grow over and back to its former state.

Roisin continued to cry. Grace went over and put an arm around her. 'You have to realise, my dear, the enormous strain your father has lived under for the last ten years, expecting at any minute that the authorities will arrive and tell us to leave.'

'I'm sorry, Dad. I did not really understand. Thank you for looking after us and can we really take the animals?'

James smiled. 'Yes you can; it is for the best.'

As soon as the paperwork was finished, Michael's men started work on the houses but first there was all the rubbish to get rid of. An agreement was reached that James, Fred and Hugh could take as much as possible of the small metal and sell it then Donald would harass the Council to get rid of the rest.

'And how many will you be building?' Michael asked Donald.

'We have permission for five. Four will be occupied at first.'

'And what about the empty one?' screamed Michael, 'I'll not be having an empty house with no rent coming in.'

'Keep your whiskers on, Michael. I will make sure you get your rent. There are plenty of travellers who need a home.'

A temporary resident was found for the empty cottage. In years to come, Roisin and Connor would marry and move in. Travellers would come from miles around to see the beautiful bride dressed in a sprigged gown with a garland of wildflowers in her hair, James proudly escorting her up the aisle of the local church. Philip and Alexa were present as guests of honour.

Michael, who provided a hog roast in the grounds of the new homestead, stopped moaning for a while about his lost income. With Donald as the taskmaster, Michael's boys built the cottages in a few months. The services were put in and they were ready for occupation. The new tenants came down to view, marvelling at the electricity, gas and main drainage.

The ladies could hardly believe it. They were about to move into a cottage with a kitchen, living room, two bedrooms and a bathroom with indoor toilet. These were simple, basic homes but luxury class compared to what they had been used to.

'I have never seen the like nor thought to do so,' said Grace with tears in her eyes.

The final job of creating a road into the new "estate" completed, James's group was set to move.

Everything from their moorland home would be removed. The fences and all the barns and containers taken down, ready to be set up on their new site. The vegetable plot was cleared and all produce saved for the winter.

Donald had arranged to run the tractor over the new site to give the women a head start and they had already been down to commence digging and planting.

The colourful original traveller's vans would be stored and hired out for fetes and film work to bring in additional revenue, a canny move arranged by Donald.

Finally, after meticulous inspection, James, Fred and Hugh were satisfied that everything had been cleared up as they were determined to leave the area as they had found it. Only the three houses in the combe would stay and could be used as overnight accommodation by walkers and hikers.

The great day for the final move arrived. Firstly horses were hitched up to the vans, then the contents, cooking pots, clothing were piled in and transported. Stella, Maggie, Siobhan and Connor, Hugh, Grace and Roisin and young James sat in the vans on their way to their new home. James and Fred went back to fetch the carts. There was sadness at leaving, mixed with gratitude for the time they had spent there.

Finally, the chickens and their coop on the cart and with the cow attached behind, James led, with Fred following, on their exit from the place they had called their home for the last ten years.

James sat erect, head held high as he guided the cart from their dwelling place on the moor for the last time. Who knew what the future held? The travellers had a new site, and it would be what they made of it.

As James guided the horses along the new road, behind the trees, one group sheltering them from the road, the other to give the big house privacy, he felt relief and gratitude that he had found his people a home.

There would be months, years of work to come but without the constant fear of being found, of going back to the nightmare of daily survival.

Epilogue

Prior to the Potato Famine, Ireland was a poverty-stricken country dependent on the potato as the primary food source. Greedy and uncaring landlords in both Ireland and England exacerbated the problem in charging high, unsustainable rents.

With the advent of the Great Hunger, the main food source was lost. The population, already frail and sick, suffered from further starvation leading on to illnesses such as typhus, scurvy, cholera, dysentery and tuberculosis. In desperation, many emigrated, mostly to America, a high proportion dying before they arrived in their new land.

Not only were the potatoes affected and left inedible but the soil was also infected. Two-thirds of the population were involved in agriculture leaving them without employment.

The government made an attempt at providing food in the form of grain but the people did not know what to do with it and the exercise was soon abandoned.

The cause of the fungus causing the famine, Herb 1, is now extinct but the effects a hundred and fifty years later live on.

A hundred years later, an official survey carried out in 1950 showed that the effects were more widespread and long-lasting than previously thought. The level of literacy was very low at the time so much of the population was unable to read the government notices on how to avoid the prevalent diseases. Mental health was damaged.

Ireland is now a flourishing and up-to-date country, not without its problems, but name a country who has none.

James Kelly, the main subject of this story, lost many relatives, his livelihood, almost his sanity which led him to try his fortune in England.

We have followed him, his family and the people who were fortunate enough to come under his care down the years. Perhaps James was wrong in taking over a small part of Dartmoor. In the end, despite the wishes of some unkind people, the group ended up in a place they can call home. James Kelly, despite the worry and everlasting need within himself to provide for others, for the survival of his family and descendants, and later others, friends, a homeless young woman in need. Surely all this wretchedness and adversity had entitled James Kelly, certainly in the view of his fellow men, a right to life.

Despite all the government regulation attempts by local councils, thousands of homeless people, not just the travellers, sleep in doorways, on the streets, in cardboard boxes every night.

So, our story ends. Many years ago, at a meeting of four old friends, Alexa sat back and waited for comments.

'You're a mug,' said Sue.

'Good on you,' said Jennie.

'Why do you always have to get involved?' asked Diana.

Good question. Why did she?

They raised their glasses to friendship.

Up on the moor, young grass grew. Small saplings began to take hold. A group of wild ponies grazed, kicked up their heels and galloped off. Rabbits scampered; a fox barked. Dartmoor was reclaiming its own.

Sometimes, on a balmy evening, James sat outside his house and looked up in the direction of the moor that had given him shelter for so many years. He had loved the life there. He looked around at his small new village and felt, not proud nor complacent, but at last content.

References

The Great Irish Famine 1845–1851 James S. Donnelly jnr. History Press, Social Science 2002

Irish Potato famine deaths. Herbert. P.H. Nusterling Historical methods – A Journal of Quantitative and Quantitative and Interdisciplinarian History vol. 42

Repeal of the Corn Laws Hansard vol. 81 – Debated June 10 1845

Repeal of the Act of Union Hansard vol. 4 Debated June 10 1845

Cornish Fishing Industry John McWilliams, Amberley Publishing

Irish Potato Famine – History Charles Rivers. Sutton publishing 2002

Thomas Hardy 1840–1928 The Mayor of Casterbridge

Dartmoor National Park Information Centre

St Just in Roseland Church, Cornwall